"Are you even for real, cowboy?"

He tugged her to her feet and pulled her into his arms. "I'm as real as it gets."

She knew he was going to kiss her. Knew she should stop him. Instead she melted into the thrill and the taste of him. Passion claimed her so completely that she literally lost her breath.

When Tague pulled away, she felt a burning in her lungs and a hunger deep inside her that she had little chance of ever satisfying.

She lay back down, turned off the light and stared at the ceiling. She needed to put what had just transpired into some kind of perspective. All she could come up with was that she was being forced to put her trust in the rugged cowboy with the boyish charm and the determination of a mad bull.

Heaven help them all.

JOANNA WAYNE

LIVE AMMO

TORONTO NEW YORK LONDON
AMSTERDAM PARIS SYDNEY HAMBURG
STOCKHOLM ATHENS TOKYO MILAN MADRID
PRAGUE WARSAW BUDAPEST AUCKLAND

Thanks to all my readers who believe in love and cowboys.
And to my family, who taught me that family
is important to every aspect of our lives.

Recycling programs
for this product may
not exist in your area.

ISBN-13: 978-0-373-69628-4

LIVE AMMO

For questions and comments about the quality of this book
please contact us at Customer_eCare@Harlequin.ca.

® and TM are trademarks of the publisher. Trademarks indicated with
® are registered in the United States Patent and Trademark Office, the
Canadian Trade Marks Office and in other countries.

www.Harlequin.com

Printed in U.S.A.

ABOUT THE AUTHOR

Joanna Wayne was born and raised in Shreveport, Louisiana, and received her undergraduate and graduate degrees from LSU-Shreveport. She moved to New Orleans in 1984, and it was there that she attended her first writing class and joined her first professional writing organization. Her debut novel, *Deep in the Bayou,* was published in 1994.

Now, dozens of published books later, Joanna has made a name for herself as being on the cutting edge of romantic suspense in both series and single-title novels. She has been on the Waldenbooks bestseller list for romance and has won many industry awards. She is also a popular speaker at writing organizations and local community functions and has taught creative writing at the University of New Orleans Metropolitan College.

Joanna currently resides in a small community forty miles north of Houston, Texas, with her husband. Though she still has many family and emotional ties to Louisiana, she loves living in the Lone Star State. You may write Joanna at P.O. Box 852, Montgomery, Texas 77356.

Books by Joanna Wayne

HARLEQUIN INTRIGUE

*Four Brothers of Colts Run Cross
‡Special Ops Texas
†Sons of Troy Ledger
**Big "D" Dads

CAST OF CHARACTERS

Tague Lambert—Youngest of the Lambert brothers. Born into a wealthy ranching and oil family, he's a cowboy at heart with no interest in settling down—until he meets Alexis Beranger.

Alexis Beranger—She's running scared, but determined to keep Tommy safe at any price.

Tommy—The precocious two-year-old loves horses and chocolate.

Carolina Lambert—Tague's mother is a woman who loves her family above all.

Durk Lambert—Tague's brother offers advice from a business trip in the Middle East.

Emma and Damien Lambert—Tague's brother and sister-in-law cut their honeymoon short to be there for Tague and Alexis.

Booker Dell Collins—Carjacker.

Detective Gerald Hampton—Dallas Police Department detective investigating the carjacking.

Scott Jeffery Hayden—Legendary detective and Alexis's ex-husband.

Lena Fox Hayden—Third wife of Scott Hayden.

Meghan Sinclair—The private detective may have shared a past with Durk Lambert.

Jackson Phelps—A retired NCIS agent, now private detective hired by Tague Lambert to help clear Alexis's name.

Bronco—Loyal bodyguard to Scott Jeffery Hayden.

Chapter One

"Hand over those keys."

Alexis Beranger spun around and stared into a pair of glassy eyes that looked as if they were popping out of the man's head.

Her heart slammed against her chest as he pushed his fetid, sweaty body against her. The man was taller than her and burly. And judging from his dilated pupils, he was also stoned.

She scanned the supermarket parking lot. The nearest people were a teenage worker herding a train of empty carts and a pregnant woman. Both were several yards away, walking in the opposite direction and oblivious to her situation.

The man closed his hand over hers. She fought back, kicking and clawing with her free hand as she yelled for help. His strength was overpowering and he easily wrenched the keys from her grasp.

He slapped her hard across the face and then silenced her with a meaty hand over her mouth.

Tommy began to wail from the backseat. She went for the man's eyeballs, clawing like a mother tiger. Her fingers missed their mark but dug bloody trenches into his face.

His hand left her mouth. "Don't make me use this, bitch. Get in the car." His voice slurred, but his body had hardened to solid steel.

That's when she saw the pistol clutched in his right hand—pointed at her son's head.

Terror swept through her, and she struggled to breathe. "Take the car. Take my purse. Take whatever you want. Just don't hurt my son."

"Want out, Mommy. Want out."

"Tell the brat to shut up."

"He's afraid. He's only two." Her voice quivered. "Let me get him out of his seat and we'll just walk away. I won't even call the cops."

"Lying bitch. Get in the *car* now!"

She heard footsteps and a woman's voice. Surely this monster would run away. Instead he punched her in the face and sent her staggering backward so hard she careened against the car parked next to hers. The back of her skull collided with the rearview mirror, waves of black scrambling her vision, and she slumped almost to the pavement before regaining her balance.

"Security! Security!" The woman's calls for help were shrill and loud enough to be heard throughout the lot.

The man jumped into Alexis's car and slammed the door behind him.

Reeling from the blow, Alexis lunged for the back door handle.

Too late. He'd locked the doors. She pounded her fists against the vehicle as the car pulled out.

The woman and a couple of young men came running over to help.

"Don't let him get away," Alexis shouted. "He has my son in that car."

"I'm calling 911," the woman said.

One of the men muttered curses. The other put a hand on Alexis's shoulder. "The cops will catch him. They won't let him get away with the kid."

"He already did!"

Alexis pushed them out of the way and took off after the car. Her only chance was for someone to see her, hear her cries, and cut off the fleeing car. No one did.

Desperate, she cut through the maze of parked cars and raced toward the nearest lot exit. She made it just in time to see the car jump the curb and spin into the busy street.

An SUV swerved to avoid crashing into her stolen sedan. Neither driver slowed down. Bordering on hysteria, she dashed into the thick of the traffic.

Brakes squealed. Curses flew at her from passing cars. The driver of a black pickup truck that had just missed running over her skidded to a stop. He opened his door and started to get out.

Before he could, she rushed to his passenger side door, yanked it open and slid into the truck. She pointed dead ahead.

"Follow that car."

Chapter Two

Tague Lambert stared at the shapely woman in the white shorts and cute little striped T-shirt who'd just jumped into his truck uninvited. Her right eye was swelling like biscuit dough in a hot oven and a nasty lump was forming on the back of her head.

He felt as if he'd just been dropped into a B movie and he was damn sure he hadn't made a casting call.

"Step on it," she ordered. "You're letting him get away."

Bossy, but frantic and obviously scared out of her wits. She looked familiar, but he couldn't place her. "Nice to meet you, too." Tague yanked the car into gear and hit the accelerator. "Who am I following?"

"That gray Honda sedan that just blew through the yellow light at the next corner."

Tague craned his neck to get a better view of the speeding car. "Who's driving?"

"The crackhead who just jumped me and stole my car."

So, she'd been carjacked. That explained a lot.

"Maybe you should go to a hospital. That Honda is not worth our getting killed."

"It is to me. My son's in that car."

"Then buckle up." Adrenaline pumping, Tague darted around a black Buick, but then lost sight of the gray sedan altogether when a panel truck changed into his lane and blocked his view. He swerved into the left lane.

A few seconds later, he caught a glimpse of the sedan a block and a half in front of them, taking the corner at breakneck speed. Another three minutes and the driver could access the interstate. Then he'd really have to stomp the pedal to the metal to keep up. It was too damn risky.

He lay on his horn and sped through a yellow light.

"Call 911," Tague ordered. "Give them our location and explain the situation."

"My phone's in the car."

"Use mine." He yanked it from his pocket and tossed it to her.

He turned the corner to the earsplitting sound of a collision. He spotted the gray sedan as it veered into a wild spin, finally winding up against the front of a vacant one-story building. The red Jeep Wrangler that it had crashed into fared little better, but at least it was still in the street.

Traffic came to a screeching halt. Wary of what he might be rushing into, Tague grabbed his pistol from beneath his seat. He hit the ground running.

From a distance, he saw the carjacker climb from the wreckage and race away from the scene. A white handbag was clutched in his right hand, doubtlessly not his.

By the time Tague reached the scene, the thief had ducked into a nearby alley. Tague lingered long enough to see a tall guy in jeans and a blue sports shirt pull the kid from the backseat of the wrecked car.

The kid wailed for his mother; there was no sign of

blood. Tague took off after the thief, pistol in hand, his senses keen to avoid being ambushed. He was used to shooting snakes in the grass, not chasing criminals.

The quick check of the alley was futile. The guy might have climbed through a broken window on one of the deserted warehouses or jumped the fence at the other end and escaped into the maze of side streets. Hunting him down was probably better left to the cops.

He returned to the scene of the accident and quickly spotted his sexy hitchhiker. She was standing in a crowd of bystanders, holding the kid in her arms.

"I don't know how to thank you," she said as Tague walked up and stopped at her elbow.

"Not sure what you'd thank me for."

"Jumping into the fray." She hugged her son tighter. "Has anyone checked on the driver of the Jeep? Is he okay?"

"He seems to be," a middle-aged brunette standing next to him chimed in. "But I called 911. I think some other people did, too. Ambulances and the police are on the way."

Approaching sirens were already screaming in the background. Gawkers scattered as a squad car arrived.

"Be right back," Tague said. He dashed over to his truck that he'd left in the middle of the street. It was blocked in tight, but he slid his pistol back into its scabbard beneath the seat and locked the vehicle. He was licensed to tote, but no need to waste time explaining all that to the cops.

He'd give a statement to the officers and then clear out so that he could take care of the business that had brought him into Dallas in the first place.

Two more squad cars rolled up, lights flashing. Four uniformed cops hit the streets.

"I need the owners of the cars and any eye witnesses," one of the other officers clipped loudly. "The rest of you need to move on so emergency personnel can go to work."

To his surprise, Tague spotted the woman, still carrying the kid, but striding away from the cops. Impulsively, he rushed to catch up with her.

"Where do you think you're going?"

"Away from the chaos so that I can take care of my son."

The boy's arms were locked tight around his mother's neck.

"Do you think he's injured?" Tague asked.

"I don't think so, but he's frightened and all the strangers and sirens aren't helping."

Maybe he'd been rash in trying to avoid getting involved. The woman still looked a bit terrified. Her eye looked none too good, either. And the lump on her head was more pronounced than before.

"You and the boy both need to be checked out by medical personnel," Tague said. "There's an ambulance on the way."

"We don't need an ambulance." She started walking away again.

Obviously she was too upset or injured to think straight. He grabbed her arm and tugged her to a stop. "You can't leave the scene of an accident without talking to the cops."

"I could if you would mind your own business."

"You didn't feel that way a few minutes ago when you

were ordering me to give chase. The least you can do is give the police a description of the carjacker."

She stopped walking and shifted the kid to her other hip. "Okay, you win. I'll talk to the cops, but I don't expect it to change anything."

The lady had an attitude problem. He'd have figured she'd be eager to describe the carjacker to the cops. It made him wonder if she didn't have other reasons for avoiding the police.

"I think it's time we met officially," he said. "I'm Tague Lambert."

"I'm Alexis."

"No last name?"

"Beranger. This is Tommy."

Tommy began to squirm. "Go home, Mommy."

"Soon, sweetie." She lowered him to the ground, but held on tight to his hand as a cop approached them.

"I'll stick around until you're done," Tague offered, his interest and curiosity piqued.

She shot him a *back off* look. "I really appreciate all you've done, but I'm fine on my own now. And I'm sure you have better things to do than broil under the midday sun with strangers."

"No. A car chase and foiling a kidnapping pretty much tops anything I had planned."

Besides, this might not be a movie shoot, but it had all the elements of one. And he'd always been a sucker for a mystery starring a sexy female lead.

"OFFICER BILLY WHITFIELD," the cop said as he stepped in front of Alexis. "One of the witnesses said that your son was in the gray Honda at the time of the collision."

"Yes."

No doubt everyone in hearing distance had figured that out from the frenzied state she'd been in when she'd rushed to the car and grabbed Tommy.

Now it was the cop who incited her panic. She had to watch every word. Tell him only what he needed to know and make sure he didn't feel the need to go digging into her background.

"Can I have your name?"

"Alexis Beranger."

"Were you driving the car?"

"No, I wasn't even in the car."

The cop turned his attention to Tommy. "Is this the boy who was involved in the collision?"

"Yes. This is Tommy."

"Lucky kid to walk away from that wreck with no serious injuries."

"It was a miracle," she agreed.

"Who was driving the car?"

"The stoned thug who stole it." A swell of renewed anger sharpened her tone.

The cop's stare intensified. "Are you telling me your car was stolen with the kid inside?"

"Yes, from the Clancy Supermarket parking lot just blocks from here."

His mouth drew into two tight lines. "In that case, we've just gone from a major traffic accident to an attempted kidnapping. Excuse me a minute. I need to call the precinct and let them know what's going on here."

Whitfield stepped away and made the call on his cell phone. Alexis took a deep breath as her insides began to roll again. The last thing she needed was yet more cops snooping into her life.

"If you know who stole the car, you should level with

the officer," Tague said, keeping his voice low enough that she doubted Whitfield had heard it.

"Are you suggesting I knew that punk?"

"I'm not suggesting anything, except that Whitfield seems to be making you awful nervous."

"It's not him that's making me nervous. It's the situation."

It also worried her that Tague's reassuring manner was so disarming. It tempted her to trust him when she knew she didn't dare.

A hammering sensation started just below her right temple as Whitfield rejoined them.

"I'll take a statement from you now," the cop said, "but a detective will be in touch with you to follow up later today."

"There's not much I can tell you or a detective. I had just gotten to the supermarket and was getting out of my car when a thug walked up and demanded my keys. I struggled, but he had muscles—and a pistol."

"Is that how you got that black eye and the knot on the back of your head?"

She reached back and felt the tender flesh swelling beneath her hair. No wonder she was getting such a headache. "I fell backward and into a rearview mirror when he punched me."

"Did you call 911?" Whitfield asked.

"I made an attempt while we were chasing after the thief. I'd just started explaining the situation when the collision occurred. I think I just dropped the phone at that point, but I don't actually remember. I was too panicked to think."

"You broke the connection. The dispatcher reported

it, but we didn't have a name or a location. We figured it was a hoax, but she was trying to get a location anyway."

The cop nodded toward to Tague. "Are you the boy's father?"

"No," Alexis said quickly, answering for him. "There is no father, at least not one who's in the picture. I'm divorced." *And please let the cop and the detective leave it at that.*

"We've just met," Tague explained. "I happened to be at the right place at the right time."

"And you are?"

"Tague Lambert."

"Any kin to the late Hugh Lambert?"

"I'm his youngest son."

The cop shifted and rubbed a spot over his right ear as his attitude did some adjusting. "Mr. Lambert was a good man. I arrested him once for speeding. I had no idea he was good friends with the chief of police. Not that I would have done anything differently, mind you."

"Of course not."

"Point is, instead of pulling rank on me and expecting favors, he sent my supervisor a letter commending me for the professional way I handed the violation."

"That was Dad," Tague said. "Praise if you deserved it. A reaming-out if you didn't."

"Like I said, a good man." Whitfield swatted at a mosquito that buzzed his ear. "Did you witness the carjacking, Mr. Lambert?"

"No. Alexis had chased the car into the middle of the street when I spotted her. I threw on my brakes to miss her. She jumped in my truck and ordered me to catch up to the Honda. I could tell she meant business, so I jumped to it."

"Trying to follow him was a smart move on your part," Whitfield said, turning his attention back to Alexis. "Had the perp not wrecked that car, no telling where he might have taken your son or what might have happened after that."

Alexis shuddered at the thought. But Tague had been there for her, a hero in jeans, boots and a cowboy hat. He might be only an urban cowboy, but he looked tanned, virile and hard-bodied enough to be the real thing. He'd be a great guy to have for a friend—had she been in a position to have friends.

Whitfield pulled a pen and a small notebook from his shirt pocket. "So tell me exactly what occurred in the parking lot, Mrs. Beranger."

Once she started relating the incident, the details poured out. She was amazed at how much she remembered considering her state of mind at the time and how fast everything had happened.

Before she finished, an ambulance arrived on the scene. The sirens sent Tommy into another meltdown. He began to scream.

She picked him up and tried to reassure him as two paramedics rushed to where they were standing, apparently at the directions of one of the other police officers.

It took her several minutes to convince them that in spite of her bruises and the bump on her head, she didn't require their assistance and neither did her wailing son.

"I'll see a doctor and I'll definitely have my son checked out," she insisted. "But putting him in an ambulance will only frighten him more. Honestly, he seemed fine before you arrived. He's crying because he's afraid of strangers and sirens, not because he's in pain."

They still had her sign a waiver asserting she'd refused their services.

"I'm sure you realize that your car will have to be towed," Whitfield said.

"I know it's not drivable."

"Since you turned down the ambulance, you should either call a friend to pick you up and take you and the boy to the nearest emergency room, or I can have an officer drive you there. I suggest the former. It would be quicker and you don't want to stand around in this heat any longer than you have to."

"I've already taken care of that," she lied. The last thing she needed was to spend any unnecessary time with a cop. Nor did she need the prying questions of emergency room personnel unless it was necessary for Tommy's well-being. Anonymity was her best protection.

Whitfield asked a few more questions and then put his notebook away.

"There's been a rash of shootings in this area lately," Whitfield continued, "all related to drugs or gang activity. Considering the violence these junkies are capable of, you're fortunate that the car is all you lost."

"Actually, I think the thief made off with her handbag," Tague said. "I got a quick glimpse of the driver when he fled the vehicle. He was holding what looked like a ladies' white purse when he disappeared into the alley. I gave chase but never spotted him again."

Alexis exhaled, blowing off steam. Now she not only had no car, she had no phone, no ready cash to call a taxi, and worst of all, no driver's license. And it wasn't as if she could just march in and request another one in

Alexis Beranger's name, since as far as she knew Alexis Beranger didn't exist.

"I can't let you in the car until it's been checked for prints," Whitfield said. "But I can see if your purse is in the vehicle."

Dread squeezed the breath from her lungs. She should have realized they'd do a routine check for fingerprints.

And when they did, they'd find hers and discover her real identity.

"How long will it take you to check for prints?" she asked

"With the backlog they have in the investigation unit, we'll be lucky if we get the report back this week."

"What's the quickest you could get it back?"

"Wednesday afternoon," Whitfield said, "but that would only be if the chief put a rush on it."

She couldn't rule that out. It was Monday now. That gave her two days to disappear again. And she had no car.

"You should go ahead and alert your insurance company," Whitfield said, "though I suspect they'll total it. The Honda is what—about eight years old?"

"Ten." She'd bought it from a used car lot in Vegas seven months ago, a few days after fleeing California. She'd have to settle for one older than that this time. Her ready cash was running low.

"I'll need Tommy's car seat before I leave today," she said.

Whitfield dabbed at the perspiration that beaded on his forehead with a wrinkled handkerchief he'd pulled from his back pocket. "I'll have one of the cops get the boy's seat for you now. Then you'll be free to go. Like

I said, a detective from the precinct will contact you, likely later today."

"My phone is in my purse," she said.

"That's okay. I need to get your home address anyway."

She provided it and a few other relative pieces of information he would have normally taken from her fake driver's license. And now she'd have a detective making a house call. Could this get any worse?

Yes, she answered herself. It could be a million times worse. Tommy might have actually been kidnapped or seriously injured or even killed in the wreck. And she was the one who'd vowed to keep him safe.

"Want to go home," Tommy whined as Whitfield walked away.

"I know you do, sweetie." He was hot and tired and recovering from a traumatic morning. And now he'd have to get used to a new home.

"Exactly how is it you called a friend when you don't have a phone?" Tague asked.

Her irritation swelled. "So now you're starting with the questions, too?"

"I'm just wondering how you plan to get home when you have no car and no money."

"I figured I could bum bus money from you."

"I never lend money to friends."

"We're not exactly friends."

"We must be. I never offer rides to strangers."

"I didn't hear you offer."

"Give me time." He made a mock bow. "May I give you a lift?"

Her ready response was *no*. But she really did need a

ride. And it wasn't as if she'd be around long enough to worry about the cowboy trying to stay in touch.

"I live on the other side of town," she cautioned. "You might want to consider that before you make those rash offers."

"In that case, I may have to charge double."

"You expect me to pay you?"

"I was kidding. Let's get out of here."

"Okay, but I have to make a stop before going home."

"At the hospital, I hope."

"If it's necessary. First I'd like to check with my son's pediatrician. If the doctor can check him out at the clinic near my house, it would be less stressful to Tommy. He's familiar with the setting and the staff."

"I can handle that. But you still need someone to check out your injuries."

"I'm fine, and if you'll stop with the questions and orders, I'll accept your offer. But just for a ride," she emphasized, just in case he was expecting more. Tague looked and acted like a gentleman, but she'd been fooled before.

"A ride was all I offered. You're safe with me, Alexis. But I can provide references if you doubt me."

"From your mother?"

"Either her or my parole officer." He put a hand up to cut off her protests before they formed. "I'm only teasing."

"Okay, cowboy. You're on."

Chapter Three

Tague thumbed through the newsmagazine for about twenty seconds before dropping it back to the waiting room table. It was his first time in a pediatrician's office since he'd been a kid himself and he felt as out of place as a wasp in a beehive.

He was the only person in the room not accompanied by a kid or two. One woman was corralling three, none of whom appeared to be old enough to go to school.

Tague had nothing against kids, but the idea of being outnumbered by them three to one was a little frightening. They seemed more work than a herd of cattle, and they definitely required more supervision.

It had to be tough raising one on your own the way Alexis was doing. Already married and divorced though Tague figured she was likely no older than his twenty-six years.

The woman was definitely intriguing. She was feisty enough to try to fight off an armed thug and then commandeer Tague into action to go after her son. But she was ready to run from a cop just trying to help.

What really had him going was that she looked so hauntingly familiar. Yet he was pretty sure he hadn't run into her before.

He couldn't help noticing her great figure and stunning legs that did terrific things for her white shorts. Straight, blond, silky hair that cupped her chin and fell to her shoulders. Enticing lips.

But it was the eyes that really mesmerized him. Sort of a blue-violet color tucked in between thick, dark lashes. Sometimes fiery. Sometimes shadowed and troubled. Always hypnotic. She was not the kind of woman a red-blooded male would forget meeting.

And the druggie who'd stolen her purse had her ID and her home address. Neither Whitfield nor Alexis had mentioned the danger that could entail, but both had to be aware of it.

Even if the detective who'd be calling on her later today brought it up, he'd only warn her to be careful and keep her doors locked. She'd be on her own if the thug decided to show up for a return engagement.

Or maybe she wouldn't be alone. She could have a jock live-in who could make the thug wish he'd kept running. But if there was a man on demand, Alexis hadn't mentioned him nor called him—at least not on Tague's phone.

That still didn't make Tague responsible for her safety. After all, it was only a bizarre act of fate that had thrown them together. The only reason he'd been on that street at all was a detour prompted by a street repair crew.

Tague had come into town this morning to pick up a saddle from the best saddle maker in Texas. Not for himself, but for his brother Damien who'd had it made as a surprise for his new wife. He wanted it to be in the tack room waiting on Emma when they returned from their honeymoon.

It was midafternoon now and Tague was yet to pick up the saddle. Alexis had insisted he didn't have to wait for her at the doctor's office. But what kind of jerk would leave a woman and a kid stranded after the morning they'd been through?

Still, he was rotten at sitting and doing nothing. He stood and left the waiting room, choosing instead to pace the wide hallway of the three-story medical complex. Even that felt confining.

He took out his phone and called Cork. With his brother Damien on his honeymoon, he relied on his head wrangler more than ever.

"How's it going?" he asked when Cork finally answered.

"Busy. Just finished moving the cattle scheduled for their injections into the holding pens. And one of the horses is acting colicky. Don't know what brought it on. There's been no change in the feed."

"Which horse?"

"King."

Damien's personal horse. "Keep an eye on King. Administer the usual treatment, but don't hesitate to call Doctor Benson if you think it's necessary."

"Will do," Cork said. "Are you heading back this way yet?"

"No, I decided last minute to take care of some other business while I'm in town. I'm not sure what time I'll get back to the Bent Pine," Tague said. "I could be late so tell Mother not to wait dinner on me."

"I'll let her know."

"If anything comes up, you can always reach me on my cell," Tague added.

"Gotcha."

While he had the phone out, he made a quick call to Harry Rucker and let him know that he might not make it to his shop to pick up the saddle today.

It was forty-five minutes of pacing later when Alexis came swinging out the door.

"Me got a sucker," Tommy said, holding up a bright red lollipop before poking it between his lips.

Alexis's brows arched. "You're still here."

"I told you I'd wait," he said.

"I know, but I thought you might reconsider and decide you'd wasted enough time on me."

"I wanted to make sure the boy is okay."

"Really? You stayed for Tommy?" Her expression registered surprise and a hint of pleasure. "I appreciate that."

"So where is my lollipop?" Tague asked.

"Sorry. You have to get examined to earn one of those."

"Maybe we can work on that later?"

Her cheeks reddened.

"Once again, only teasing," Tague said. "I'm just here to taxi you home." He opened the door and they walked out of the waiting room together, Tommy sucking for all he was worth and holding fast to his mother's hand.

Once Tommy was safely buckled into the backseat, Alexis climbed into the front seat with Tague.

Tague started the engine. "I'll need directions."

"Take a left when you leave the parking lot, then a right at the second light. My apartment complex is two miles down on the right. It takes up two blocks. You can't miss it."

"That would have been a long walk in this heat."

"Ten steps is a long walk in this heat. I'm sure I would

have opted for a taxi. I have cash at home that I could have paid him with."

"Did the doctor give Tommy a good report?"

"He said he'll have some bruising where the safety belt dug into his shoulder and on at least one of his legs. The flesh is already turning purple. But Dr. Pendleton detected no signs of internal injuries or sprains."

"That's great and incredible, especially seeing the condition of your Honda."

"I know. I hate to even think about how close we skirted tragedy."

"My mother would say that angels saw Tommy through the danger," Tague said.

"I think I'd like your mother."

Unfortunately, the thief had also been uninjured and able to flee the scene.

Alexis turned toward the backseat to check on Tommy. "Remind me when we get to my house and I'll clean the sticky handprints from your seat."

"Absolutely. Can't have you messing up my work truck. Cows wouldn't like it."

Alexis wrinkled her nose. "You don't really put cows in here, do you?"

"Not in the cab. And speaking of bruising, you have a nice range of ugly colors painting your eye."

She pulled down the visor and checked her reflection in the mirror. "Pretty hideous, isn't it?"

"I wouldn't go that far. Did the doctor say what you should do for that?"

"Put ice on it. In fact, his nurse had me keep a cold pack on it while I waited for the doctor to see Tommy."

"What about that bump on your head?"

"He thinks I should have gone to the emergency

room, but since I didn't, and since I'm not having any problems with coherence, balance or unusual pain, he says I should just watch for symptoms of a concussion. In other words, it's no big deal."

"So you both got good reports. That should relieve your mind."

"The only thing that could make it better would be to learn that the thief looks even worse after wrecking my car than I do."

Once Tague had turned the corner, he spotted a supermarket on the right.

"You never got your groceries," he said. "Do you want to stop now?"

"Thanks, but I can get what I need later."

"Why wait? You have a vehicle and a guy to tote the bags now. Unless you have a handy man at your disposal."

"I don't have any man at my disposal, handy or otherwise."

The answer pleased him, though it shouldn't have. It wasn't like he was going to stick around for more than a day. They were strangers. He was helping out in a crunch.

The fact that she was fascinating and a temptress even with her black eye didn't mean he was looking to start parking his boots under her bed or even pop in for a beer on occasion. Not that she'd invited him.

He pulled into the supermarket lot and found a spot near the front door.

Alexis looked around cautiously as he parked, as if she half expected the monster who'd attacked her earlier to show up for a rematch.

"I don't have any money with me," she reminded him as she opened her car door.

"I do."

"I'll pay you back when we get to my house," she said.

"Better than that, you can fix me a sandwich. I missed lunch and I'm famished."

"I should provide more than a sandwich after all you've done," she said, "but to tell you the truth, I'm a lousy cook."

"Now you tell me after I've wasted a whole day on you."

"Whoa, cowboy. I never asked you to do…"

"Just trying to ease a little of the tension that's got you gripping my door handle so tight, you're liable to dent it."

He was beginning to think it wasn't only cops she mistrusted, but men in general.

She exhaled slowly. "I am a little uptight."

"And you have every right to be. But you're safe now, so let's go buy some groceries."

"Want kokalat," Tommy said, as she released the catch on his safety belt.

"I don't think you need chocolate," she said. "You just had a lollipop."

"All gone. Want kokalat," he said, unperturbed by reason.

"You can choose a chocolate bar for later, but you can't open it until after dinner," Alexis said as they started toward the door.

Tommy walked between them until they reached the lines of empty carts. Then Alexis swung him up and settled him in the child seat, buckling him in so that he couldn't crawl or fall out.

It struck Tague how much they must look like a typical family out shopping.

The thought terrified him. He walked away from Alexis as soon as they entered the store, shopping alone to buy a few items, including a couple of steaks, two baking potatoes and a nice bottle of wine. Alexis could use a glass after the day she'd had. And he hadn't been kidding about being starved. A sandwich wouldn't cut it.

"TOMMY'S FALLEN ASLEEP," Alexis said when they arrived at her apartment with the few groceries she'd bought. "I should have known he was being too quiet."

She shifted Tommy's head to a more comfortable position and then unbuckled his safety belt before lifting him into her arms.

"Why don't you let me carry him in for you?" Tague offered.

"I can handle him."

"I wouldn't feel too manly following you up the stairs empty-handed while you're lugging a sleeping kid."

"You'd be lugging groceries."

"A carton of milk, a loaf of bread and a kokalat bar?"

"I bought more than that."

"Not much."

Because she'd be leaving town before the detective had his fingerprints and she'd be traveling light. And if Tague really knew her, he'd be running for the hills instead of offering to hang around.

"Far be it for me to offend the manhood of my chauffeur," she said, handing Tommy over.

A niggling uneasiness crept deep inside her as Tommy stirred and then resettled with his head resting against Tague's chest. It was the first time any man had held him since they'd fled Los Angeles in the middle of a dark, smoke-filled night.

She reached into the backseat for the groceries.

"Just get the chocolate so it doesn't melt," Tague said. "I'll come back for the rest as soon as I put Tommy down."

"I can easily manage two bags."

"And leave my six-pack to boil? Besides, you've got to come up with a key. Do you have one hidden somewhere or will you need to have a manager let you in?"

"I'll need to have a key reissued." She would have never risked leaving a key where it could be found. She grabbed her two bags of groceries. The beer could stay where it was and go home with Tague.

She didn't have time for company now. She had to find a way to get her hands on a vehicle that would get her out of town.

Tague stared at the three flights of stairs.

"I'm on the second floor," she said. "Apartment 212, just up those steps and turn right at the top." She motioned to the covered walkway that ran from one corner of the building to the other. "Two doors down. There's an elevator at the west end of the building, but I never take it."

"No wonder you're in such terrific shape."

She turned to hide the unexpected blush that burned in her cheeks. It was just an offhanded compliment. It shouldn't have affected her at all, especially with all she had on her mind.

Tague started toward the stairs.

"You should probably go with me to the leasing office so that you can wait in the air-conditioning," she said.

"It may take a few minutes to get a key. It all depends on how busy they are."

"We're right behind you."

She hurried to the first-floor office. Fortunately, one of the leasing agents was readily available and eager to accommodate. Alexis only told her she'd lost the keys, omitting any reference to the carjacking incident.

Once she had a replacement key in hand, she climbed the stairs with Tague at her side. The day's developments, including his presence, were mind-boggling.

A day that had started out as normal—or at least as normal as any of Alexis's days ever were—had quickly deteriorated. When that thug had driven off with Tommy, the terror had consumed her. The same way it had when another maniac had threatened Tommy's life.

That fear still haunted her every waking moment and created a never-ending nightmare. No hunky cowboy had ever ridden to the rescue in that nightmare. And no matter how genial and accommodating Tague seemed, she didn't dare trust him to play that role now.

They were almost up the stairs when she noticed an unfamiliar man leaning against the railing near her door. Tall, with red hair, a modest paunch, and ruddy skin. His stance and stare were intimidating.

Her muscles tensed and her arm tightened about the bags she was carrying, forcing a couple of oranges over the rim of the paper bag. They rolled for a few seconds before bouncing their way down the stairs like squishy orange balls.

"Are you Alexis Beranger?"

She left his question unanswered. "Who are you?"

"Detective Gerald Hampton with the Dallas Police Department." He flashed a badge and an ID. "I understand your vehicle was carjacked and then wrecked today."

Her muscles relaxed until she was no longer grinding her teeth. "I was a carjacking victim, but I've already told Officer Whitfield all I know."

"I've seen Whitfield's report," Hampton said. "But I'd still like to talk to you. This shouldn't take more than a half hour."

She juggled the groceries so that she could poke her key into the lock.

Keep cool, she reminded herself. Don't do anything to arouse suspicions. She was the victim, not a suspect. She had to keep it that way.

Amazingly, the conversation didn't wake Tommy. Apparently the day had taken a lot out of him, as well. "Just have a seat anywhere," she said, as they entered the small and sparsely furnished living area. "I'll put my son to bed so that he can finish his nap."

Tague followed her to the bedroom and lay Tommy in his toddler bed. When she bent over her son, her arm brushed Tague's. Awareness created a quivering sensation in her stomach. Was she now so desperate for a man to lean on that even a kind act affected her senses?

"Thanks," she whispered as she backed away from the bed. "You handled putting him down like a pro. He didn't even open an eye."

"Beginner's luck," he assured her once they'd stepped into the narrow hallway. "Only kid I've been around is my brother and sister-in-law's foster daughter Belle and she's only a few months old."

Alexis started back to the living area, but Tague stepped in her path. He leaned in so close she felt his warm breath on her neck. The quivery sensations in the pit of her stomach became more intense.

"Are you nervous about talking to the detective or am I misreading something?"

"I don't know what you're talking about."

"You were literally shaking when you spotted him outside your door."

"It's just been a very difficult day."

"I can sit in on your meeting with the detective, if you like."

"It's not necessary." In fact, it was downright dangerous.

At this point, Tague was likely a bigger threat to her anonymity than the detective was.

Yet, the truth was, she didn't want him to leave her alone with a man who might recognize her at any moment and pull out his cuffs. Tague might only be a pseudo friend, but that was better than nothing.

"Stick around if you want, though," she said. "I promised you a sandwich. Wouldn't want to send you back to your cows on an empty stomach."

"Good thinking. I'll grab the rest of the groceries before they spoil in the heat and be right back."

He gave her hand a quick squeeze. He was nice to have around. Nonetheless, when he left today, she'd have to make sure their bond was irreparably severed.

She joined the detective in the living room, choosing a chair opposite where he sat on the worn sofa she'd picked up at a secondhand store.

"I'd like you to start at the beginning and tell me exactly what happened, step by step, leaving nothing out no matter how insignificant it may seem," the detective urged.

"I've already done that."

"Sometimes people remember more after the crisis is over. Every detail is important. We can't get the carjacker off the street unless we can identify him."

"You'll have fingerprints," Alexis said, all too aware of how damaging that would be.

"We can't count on that. It's a lot more difficult to get usable prints than you'd think from watching TV crime shows."

That offered little consolation. Her prints were undoubtedly all over the car. Some were surely distinct. She went through the particulars again. "I tried to scratch his eyes out," she admitted. "I brought blood and I'm sure I left scars."

"Did you tell Whitfield that?"

"I think so. I don't remember."

"It's not in his report," Hampton said. "But it is important. It's possible you have traces of the perpetrator's DNA under your fingernails."

She studied her nails, but could see nothing beneath the hot-pink polish she'd applied herself. "I've washed my hands several times since the incident."

"There could still be DNA under the nails. I have a kit in my car that will collect even small fragments of skin. I'll take care of that once we're through talking."

"So you actually have no ideas about the carjacker's identity?" she asked.

"Did you think that we would? Your description was vague."

"It happened too fast for me to register a lot of pertinent details, but the guy was stoned and a thug. You must have arrested him on other charges in the past."

"It's possible. We suspect he's a member of a neighborhood gang known as the Death Knights. They're suspected of several drive-by shootings and instances of violence over the past twelve months."

"But no one's been convicted?"

"No, because no matter how many people witness the crime, no one will testify against them," Hampton said.

"Why not?"

"Fear of being put on the Death Knight's target list."

Tague stepped into the room. "So you're hoping Alexis will do that for you."

Alexis had no idea how much Tague had heard, but apparently enough that he'd gotten the gist of the discussion.

Detective Hampton leaned forward, his elbows propped on his knees. "I hope Mrs. Beranger will have the courage to testify—or at least try to pick the carjacker out of a lineup."

"I'll help if I can," she lied. She wouldn't be around that long.

The detective turned to Tague, scrutinizing him as if he were a suspect—or at the least a troublemaker. "Are you a friend of Mrs. Beranger's?"

"You could say that. I was with her at the scene of the wreck."

Hampton studied his notes. "Tague Lambert?"

"That's right."

Hampton leveled his stare at Tague. "I'm surprised you're still here. Whitfield's report indicates you and Alexis never met before today."

"Alexis needed a ride. I provided it. I don't find that unusual."

Hampton worried a frayed spot at the edge of his pants' pocket. "Texans do tend to help their neighbors.

You may want to stay in the picture awhile longer. I have good news and bad."

"Good news would be that you apprehended the car-jacker," Alexis said.

"It's not quite that good," Hampton admitted, "but we did locate your handbag. It had been tossed into some shrubbery about two blocks from where the wreck occurred."

"Was my wallet in it?"

"No wallet and no keys, but your phone was still in the side zip compartment. The handbag is being held for evidence at the present time, but I rescued the phone for you. I figured you might need it." He took it from his pocket and handed it to her.

"Thanks."

"So the armed druggie who attacked her still has the keys to her house and her wallet with her ID and address," Tague said.

"That's the bad news," the detective said.

"What kind of protection do you propose to provide?"

Hampton looked a tad indignant. "We've alerted the patrol team for this area. They'll keep close watch on your apartment, Mrs. Beranger. If you hear or see anything suspicious, call 911 and officers will be here in a matter of minutes. If you have a friend you could stay with or who could stay with you for a few days, that's not a bad idea, either."

No, but having cops watch her house was a horrible idea. That would make sneaking away in the night all but impossible.

"I won't be staying here tonight," she said. "I've already made arrangements to stay with a girlfriend."

"That's probably the best solution," Hampton agreed.

"By the way, we need your place of employment for our records."

"I'm currently unemployed."

"If it wasn't a job that took you to that specific part of the city this morning, why were you there?"

"Horrid luck. But it was job related. I was planning to put in my application at stores in the mall near where the car was stolen," she lied.

"Had you been to that market before?"

"No."

"Then we can rule out that you were a targeted victim rather than a random one."

"I'm sure I was random."

"You might want to find a safer area to go job hunting after this," the detective said. "And a safer place to shop."

She didn't care for his insinuation. "Are you suggesting that I deliberately took my son into a risky area?"

"I'm just saying you should be aware of your surroundings."

Now he was starting to piss her off. "That market looked perfectly safe. The parking lot was full of cars. I saw other women with children. Is it not safe for them, either? If that's the case, the DPD should do a better job of policing the area or put up signs saying Unsafe for Lone Female Shoppers."

"That's the first incident of a carjacking or violence in that particular parking lot," Hampton said, going on the defensive. "I'm heading up a newly formed task force to clean up the area. And I will apprehend your carjacker," he said. "Count on it. But we can't work miracles overnight."

"Maybe not, but you'd best make some headway quick if you don't want to lose lives."

"The department is aware of that." Hampton stood and rocked back on his heels. "Now if you'll walk down to the car with me, Mrs. Beranger, I can scrape beneath your nails and have the findings checked for possible DNA of the suspect."

"I'll be happy to accompany you."

Suffocating heat smacked her in the face as she opened the door, but that was nothing compared to the fire-breathing urgency that filled her lungs as she followed Detective Hampton back to his vehicle.

He was the leader of the task force. His reputation was on the line. Nothing was going to get past him. Not even her.

She had to find a vehicle to use for her escape and she had to find it fast. Right now, her only option might lie with the cowboy who smelled of musk and pine and swaggered like a man who was incredibly comfortable in his own hunky body.

By the time she returned to the apartment, Tague had steaks sizzling beneath her broiler. She checked them out.

"Where did these come from? I was only going to make you a peanut butter and jelly sandwich."

"I did some shopping of my own while we were in the market. I also got potatoes to cook in the microwave."

"I'll wash them and get them started."

"First, can you get me a corkscrew? The wine I bought probably needs to breathe."

"Why did you buy wine? It's not as if this is a celebration."

"I thought it might help settle your nerves. But you don't have to drink it."

"Maybe just a glass. There's a corkscrew in that top drawer just in front of you."

As the odors filled the room, her stomach reminded her that it had been almost twenty-four hours since she'd supplied it with food.

She never ate breakfast and while she'd fed Tommy his lunch before they left the house, she'd merely had another cup of coffee while she'd studied her city map.

"How do you like your steak?" Tague asked.

"Free and cooked by someone else," she admitted. "And medium rare."

"Good. Judging from your lack of body fat, I was afraid you only ate carrots and lettuce on tasteless diet bread."

"I can make a meal of that," she admitted. "But I'm not opposed to a good steak."

While the potatoes cooked, she set the table and then put out the sour cream and grated cheese Tague had picked up at the market. The guy thought of everything.

And he had a great truck—a truck she desperately needed to make her getaway. Maybe she could just take it. How difficult could a carjacking be if a man who was stoned out of his mind could do it?

"Are you really looking for a job?" Tague asked, jerking her back to sanity—at least for the moment.

"I am. Do you have one for me?"

"Do you have any experience as a wrangler?"

"I rode a horse once." Actually, she hadn't, but she was supposed to. A double took over when she'd panicked in the saddle.

"Once won't cut it. But my brother could probably find you a position with his company."

"Baling hay?"

"Nothing that glamorous. But he's always looking for good office personnel. Only problem is he's in the Middle East right now negotiating a very important merger."

"What's his company?"

"Lambert Exploration and Drilling. It's a major subsidiary of Lambert Inc."

That got her attention.

"Have you heard of it?" Tague asked.

"I've heard of it." Anyone in Dallas who'd ever picked up a local newspaper or watched the evening news had heard of it. The company was not only a major player in the international oil scene, but was a major contributor to the Dallas arts and charitable organizations. "So you're one of the filthy rich Lamberts?"

"I wouldn't call us filthy—well, except when I've been shoveling manure."

"But definitely among the city's elite. Yet I don't recall seeing you grace the society pages of *The Dallas Morning News*."

"I'm not the gala type. Tux trapped me in a stranglehold once and thought I'd never break free. But I'm not completely without fame. I did get quoted in the Cattleman's Association newsletter last month."

"Thank God. I'm sure you said something brilliant."

"I can have it printed on a T-shirt for you if you like," he teased.

"I can hardly wait."

Too bad she wouldn't be around long enough to get it. One of the wealthiest men in Texas was basically slumming in her kitchen. Under other circumstances, it would have been great fun to check him out.

Now he was simply her get-out-of-town-free card—or he could be if she played this right. But she couldn't make mistakes. If Tague found out who she was, he'd turn her over to the authorities even faster than he'd come to her rescue.

Neither of them talked much once they began eating. Her stomach was still uneasy, but she managed to get down most of the steak and a few bites of the nuked potato. Yet even with a full stomach, she couldn't figure out her next move.

Tague wiped his mouth on the napkin and took a gulp of his cold beer. "You really remind me of someone, Alexis, and it's bugging me that I can't place who."

"It's the black eye," she said. "It gives me that familiar girl-next-door look."

"The girl next door to me is seventy, walks with a cane and has gray hair. Trust me, you look nothing like her."

Just her luck. Apparently Tague had seen one of her three box-office failures. He might be the only one in Dallas who had.

She was building up courage to ask to borrow his truck when her cell phone jangled. Probably Detective Hampton with more questions.

She rushed to the living room to grab her phone before it woke Tommy. He'd slept long enough, but she needed a few more minutes alone with Tague.

"Hello."

No response.

"Hello."

She heard breathing on the line. Her palms began to sweat. "Who is this?"

Still no response. She started to shake.

"What do you want?"

"You know what I want, Melinda."

Her blood ran cold as the sound of Scott Jeffery Hayden's voice burned into her soul.

Chapter Four

The phone slipped through Alexis's fingers and clattered to the living room floor. Her face was a ghostly white and she looked so unsteady that Tague feared she was about to faint. He rushed across the room and pulled her into his arms.

She shuddered, but didn't pull away. Her silky hair brushed his chin and a fierce need ripped through him. Unexpected. Unwanted. Damned untimely.

"Who was on the phone?" he demanded.

"I don't know. He didn't give his name."

"What did he say?"

"Nothing. I just heard his breathing." She drew a jagged breath.

"Son of a bitch. Have you gotten calls like that before?"

"No. It has to be the carjacker. He must have gotten my number from information in my wallet."

Tague's muscles knotted. He would love to get his hands on that guy for about two seconds. If the rotten jerk called anyone after that, he'd be talking in soprano.

"I'm not leaving here tonight until you do, Alexis. It's not safe for you or Tommy."

But he would go to his truck and retrieve his trusty

pistol. Sometimes that was the only language a man on drugs understood, especially one bent on violence. Not that calling meant he'd actually show up at Alexis's door, but even the detective hadn't ruled that out.

Alexis pulled away, then tilted her head to meet Tague's gaze. Fear shrouded her eyes, but determination pulled her face into tight, tense lines.

"I need a vehicle to get to my friend's house, but I doubt anyone will rent to me without a valid driver's license."

"Your insurance company can make arrangements for you to get a car in the morning."

"That won't help me tonight. I hate to ask you for another favor, Tague, but I'm desperate. If you'd drive me to the rental agency and get one in your name, I'd turn it back in the first thing in the morning. I'll pay you for the day's rental rate in advance."

He could do better than that. He could get her any vehicle she wanted with a phone call—a car and a driver for that matter. The company had a contract with a local transportation service they used mostly for foreign executives when visiting Dallas.

He could get her a car. Be on his way. Chalk this off as an interesting day with a supermodel-type mother who'd fallen into a heap of trouble.

That would be the sensible choice.

But he wasn't the type who could just walk away and leave her to fend for herself against a criminal.

"I have a better idea," he said. "Call Detective Hampton and let him know about the phone call. Then get your things together. I'll drive you wherever you want to go."

"Please, just do this my way," she pleaded. Desperation clung to every syllable.

The suspicions kicked back in. "There's no friend, is there?"

She hugged her arms around herself and stared at her feet. "No friend except you," she admitted. "I need this favor, Tague. Please. I wouldn't ask except I have to keep Tommy safe."

"I'll help," he said, "but only if we do this my way. I'll either stay here with you or you can go back to the Bent Pine Ranch with me."

She hesitated, and her lips stretched into tight, unsmiling lines. "I don't like being around strangers."

"If there's no friend for you to stay with, then wherever you go, you'll be around strangers. You may as well take your chances with me and my family."

"Tell me about the ranch," she whispered in a shaky voice.

"We raise cattle and horses just like almost every other Texas ranch."

"Is it near Dallas?"

"It's south of town, thirty minutes from the Dallas city limits but a world apart."

"Do you live alone?"

"Far from it. There's my mother, Carolina Lambert."

"The sophisticated socialite whose picture is in *The Dallas Morning News* on a regular basis?"

"That's Mom."

"I never pictured her living on a ranch."

"Really? I can't imagine her living anywhere else. And there's Aunt Sybil and her infamous black wig that we all swear was once a mutant animal. And Grandma Pearl—who entertains us all, especially when she doesn't wear her hearing aids. That's most of the time."

"Sounds like an interesting group."

"We're dysfunctional at its most endearing best. My brother Damien and his wife live at the Bent Pine, as well, but they're currently honeymooning in Paris."

"I think I read about their wedding in the newspaper. It was a small affair in a quaint chapel, attended by only family and close friends."

"You are into that society hoopla, aren't you?"

"Just since I moved to Dallas. I like checking out the Texas spin on life."

"We do have our own way of doing things. I hate to disappoint you, but there won't be any shindigs tonight. Mother's playing grandmother to Damien and Emma's five-month-old foster daughter, Belle, in their absence. Belle is the princess around which the Lambert household revolves."

"And you all actually live under one roof?"

"Yep, usually in harmony, though it can get off-key at times."

"How big is this house?"

"Big enough that you and Tommy can have your own small suite if that's what you're worried about. You'll have your privacy and you won't be putting anyone out."

"What will your mother say when you show up with a pair of strays?"

"'Welcome to the Bent Pine Ranch,' and then she'll set about making sure you're comfortable. She trademarked Texas hospitality."

"Then she won't be upset?"

"She'll be thankful that you don't have to be 'de-fleaed' like most of the strays I show up with."

"Then I have just one more question, Tague."

"Fire away. I'm an open book." Which he was pretty sure *she* wasn't.

"Why are you sticking your neck out like this to help me when you know absolutely nothing about me?"

"You got me there. But I don't have a lot of rules when it comes to living, Alexis. I go with my gut instincts more often than not."

"And what do your gut instincts tell you about me?"

"That you love your son enough that you'd do anything to protect him. And that you're running scared."

"Good instincts. I'll get packed and be ready to go in a matter of minutes."

"There's no rush."

But apparently there was for her. She turned and practically ran to the bedroom. He'd best call and give notice to his mom.

CAROLINA PLACED BELLE in her play seat. Belle immediately began to kick and babble and hit at the dangling toys strung across the chair that rocked a bit with her every jerky movement.

Carolina missed Damien and Emma, but she loved every minute of caring for Belle. At five months, she was a constant ball of energy and had developed quite a personality.

Carolina was already so attached to her that it would be pure agony to give her up—when and if Belle's biological father was ever found.

Neither the police nor the detective Damien hired had discovered any new leads and Carolina was beginning to think the man might have moved from the Dallas area.

Carolina couldn't help but think of Belle as her granddaughter. Her *first* granddaughter. She hoped for many more and some grandsons, too.

"You like your chair, don't you, little princess?"

Belle agreed with a smile as her tiny fingers closed around the point of a soft plastic starfish.

"You play, and I'll throw together a salad to go with our leftovers. But no baked chicken for you. You get yummy pureed fruit and a couple of spoons of baby cereal before your bottle."

Belle definitely brought much-needed joy into the house, but the evenings after her bedtime were incredibly lonely for Carolina—even when the rest of the family was around.

It had only been six months since her husband had been killed in the crash of his private plane, and she still found herself listening for his booming voice and his boisterous laughter.

But the worst was when she crawled into their empty bed at night. She ached to feel Hugh's arms around her. Missed the rhythmic sound of his breathing. Hungered for one of his teasing kisses that wrapped her world in love.

She'd love and miss him forever, but she prayed that someday the heartbreak might not be quite so poignant or so constant.

The house phone rang and she answered at the kitchen extension.

"Is this the Bent Pine Restaurant?"

"Yes," she responded. "Tonight's menu is chicken baked in a savory wine sauce, buttered baby corn and a salad made from summer greens picked this morning from the restaurant's private garden."

"Leftovers, huh?"

"Yes, there was so much chicken left from last night's supper that I gave Alda the evening off. She deserved it since she spent the afternoon helping me make plum preserves."

"Homemade preserves and giving the cook the night off. You are definitely in a domestic mood. Did Cork tell you I probably wouldn't be home for dinner?"

"Yes, but he didn't say why."

"I drove into town to pick up Emma's new saddle and ended up in a wild car chase in pursuit of a carjacker."

"Now, why are you really late?"

"Long story. I'll fill in the details later."

"There's not a problem, is there?"

"Not with me."

"Are you staying in town tonight?"

"Nope. In fact I'll be headed that way in a few minutes. I'm bringing company."

"Who?"

"Alexis Beranger and her son, Tommy."

The names did not sound familiar. "Have I met them before?"

"No, but you'll like them. Like I said, I'll explain everything when we get there. I just wanted to give you a heads-up."

"How old is her son?"

"He's a toddler. Don't go to any trouble, Mom. And don't worry about food. Alexis and I had either a very late lunch or a very early dinner, according to whose timetable you're on."

"What about the boy? Has he eaten?"

"I'm sure Alexis will take care of that. If she needs anything special for him, we'll pick it up on the way."

Something didn't add up. "Was there actually a carjacking?"

"Yes, but no one was hurt—except for a black eye and a bump on the head."

"Are you sure you're all right, Tague?"

"I'm sure. It's not even my eye that's black. Gotta run now. Later."

Carolina cradled the receiver a few seconds before hanging up the phone. If Tague had a girlfriend with a toddler son, that was news to her. Her guess was he didn't. Tague wasn't big on secrets.

But she'd never heard him mention anyone by the name of Alexis and she certainly didn't know what to make of the carjacking comment.

"Who was that on the phone?" Grandma Pearl asked as she stepped into the kitchen.

"It was Tague. He called to say he was bringing a woman home with him."

"Bringing the wash home? Where's it been?" She chuckled as she got herself a glass of water from the tap.

Obviously she'd left her hearing aids back in her room. "Not the wash, Grandma, a woman and her young son."

"Tague? Bringing a female home to meet the family? You must have heard him wrong."

"He didn't say that Alexis was a girlfriend, just that she would be spending the night."

"Hope you told him that you don't put up with any hanky-panky in this house."

"If he had hanky-panky on his mind, I'm sure he would have stayed in town."

Tague was twenty-six and Carolina had no illusions that he was a virgin. But he wasn't the playboy type, either. He worked hard and played hard, but serious relationships or marriage seemed to be the furthest thing from his mind.

But that could change in a heartbeat. It had for her the first time she'd looked up and saw Hugh smile.

TAGUE SET THE safety on his pistol and secured it to his belt holster beneath his shirt. Then, after taking another wary look around the premises, he took the stairs back to Alexis's apartment.

Like his brothers, Tague was an excellent marksman. His father had seen to that. Still, Tague had no desire to shoot it out with the bastard who'd made that intimidating phone call to Alexis. But in a case of defense, he figured he was up to the task.

However, he would love to connect with a few uppercuts to the body of the sneaky bastard. Let the thug see what it was like to pick on a man instead of woman.

But there had been no sign of anyone lurking around the apartment or the parking lot. The carjacker was probably across town, holed up in some dingy room, getting high on drugs he'd bought with the money from Alexis's wallet. The phone call was probably just to get his rocks off.

He closed the door behind him and jerked to attention at the sound of a door or drawer being slammed in Alexis's bedroom. She walked out before he could check on her. Tommy was a step behind.

"Do you need any assistance?" he asked.

"It would help if you could keep Tommy occupied for a few minutes. He woke up as soon as I started packing."

Of course he had. Who could sleep with a demolition crew on the premises?

Alexis leaned over until she was eye level with

Tommy, flashing cleavage that rocked Tague back on the heels of his boots.

"I want you to stay in here with Mr. Lambert, Tommy, while Mommy packs our luggage for a fun trip."

"Don't wanna go."

"You'll like it, I promise."

"There will be horses," Tague volunteered.

"No." Tommy wrapped his arms about Alexis's hips and peeked out from behind a shapely thigh. "Don't wanna."

"He always says no," Alexis said. "It goes with being two. Stay with Mr. Lambert," she said again, this time with authority.

Tague experienced a pang of panic. "What am I supposed to do with him?"

"Get one of the *Sesame Street* videos out of the basket next to the TV and play it for him. He loves Big Bird."

Tommy apparently liked that prospect. He let go of his mother's leg and ran to the sofa as fast as his short legs would carry him, his arms out as if he were a plane—or a big bird.

"Big Bird," Tommy called, as Alexis flicked on the TV and then left to go back to her noisy packing.

Tague got the DVD started and then paced the small room as Tommy settled in to watch the show. He was glad they'd opted to go to the ranch instead of his spending the night here. He had nothing against the apartment—except claustrophobia.

He'd never met a true cowboy who could tolerate closed-in spaces for long. Like his dad used to say, if you can see your neighbor's house from yours, you live too damn close.

Still a bit uneasy about what he was getting into,

Tague pulled out his iPhone and looked "Alexis Beranger" up on Google. There were several people by that name. None appeared to be the gorgeous young mother in the next room who was feverishly packing to go home with him. No Facebook account. No Twitter account.

But at least he knew she wasn't wanted by the cops. Whitfield might have let her slide, but he was pretty sure Detective Hampton would have run her through the system. Just being an apparent victim wouldn't have convinced a hard-nosed detective that she was a random hit and not connected to the perp.

Tommy slid off the sofa and started gyrating to the beat of the background music on the video. Well, not exactly to the beat, but he was making a stab at it. He was a cute kid, but Tague saw no real resemblance between him and his mother.

He walked over to a round lamp table and studied the selection of small framed pictures. They were all of Tommy at various ages from birth to the present. No one else was in any of the pictures, though some looked as if another person or the background had been cropped out.

Evidently the kid's dad was a father *non grata*.

Alexis poked her head into the room. "How are you at zipping overflowing suitcases?"

"Haven't had a lot of practice. I travel light, but I'll give it a try." He joined her in the bedroom and stared in disbelief. Not one but two extra-large suitcases were brimming over with clothes that looked as if they had just been pulled from hangers and thrown in. Two large shopping bags were also nearing capacity.

Her closet was empty. So were the dresser drawers that had been left open. And she'd done all that in less than thirty minutes. She was definitely in a rush to get out of here.

"Exactly how long are you planning to be on the run?"

"As long as necessary. I'm not coming back here until the carjacker is behind bars."

"That could be any day now."

"But it might not be for weeks—or ever."

From the looks of this room, she'd already decided to leave for good. "Don't you think that completely uprooting your life is a little overkill at this point?"

Her hands flew to her hips and her eyes flashed fire. "Have you ever been brutally attacked by a maniac, Tague Lambert?"

"No."

"Well, I have. Tommy and I barely escaped with our lives, and I have no intention of standing by and letting another lunatic put me or him through that kind of hell. So don't tell me about overreacting."

She opened another drawer and began tossing its contents into a shopping bag. "Feel free to renege on your offer of a ride if you think I'm unbalanced. I'll call a taxi if it comes to that. But I am leaving this house tonight."

That much was perfectly clear.

She started to march from the room. Tague grabbed her arm and tugged her to a stop.

"I'm not backing out on the offer, Alexis. I'll load the whole house if that's what you want, even if it means renting a moving van. But I get the feeling there's something more going on here."

"I was threatened by a criminal. Isn't that enough?"

"You said he didn't say anything."

"He didn't, but he called to frighten me. That tells me all I need to know."

But not all *he* needed to know. "What about calling Tommy's father? If you think your son is in danger, I think you should let his father know."

"His father is not a part of our lives."

The bitterness seemed to spring from deep inside her.

"Was it Tommy's father who attacked you?"

She closed her eyes. When she opened them again, they were moist with unshed tears. "Yes, but please don't ask me anything else about him, Tague. I'm trying hard to put that part of my life behind me."

But not doing a good job at it. "Where is Tommy's father now?"

"I have no idea. He moves around a lot and we have no contact."

"Did you press charges against him when he attacked you?"

"Will you please just let it go, Tague?" Desperation clung to every syllable.

"For now, if that's the way you want it."

"It is. And after tonight, I'll take all my past and current problems and get out of your life for good. I'll rent a car first thing in the morning and move on."

For reasons too complex and confusing to think about, he was not looking forward to that.

BOOKER DELL COLLINS stared into the dingy mirror over the stained porcelain washbasin in the cheap motel just outside the Fort Worth city limits. He hadn't dared go back home after wrecking the stolen Honda.

Even if the woman hadn't given the cops his description, they would have shown up at his house to question him. Any time there was a crime committed on his turf, cops couldn't wait to track down him and the other leaders of the Death Knights. The stinkin' police were determined to tie something on them that would stick.

They never would on Booker. For the most part, the cops played by the rules. Booker Dell had no friggin' rules and no boundaries. That's what made him invincible.

He'd killed more than once to silence an eyewitness, but with his reputation, all he had to do most of the time was threaten. The slut who'd scratched up his face wouldn't get off that light.

He ran his fingers down the angry open wound that ran from the corner of his right eye all the way to his bloody lip. The left side of his face was even worse. Her fingernails had missed that eye altogether but had dug so deep across his cheek that flesh hung from the wound like raw hamburger.

She'd have never gotten the chance to claw at him if he hadn't been stoned half out of his mind on crack. Tatum's crack, the best money could buy. And last night Booker Dell had carried enough of the green stuff to buy a month's supply.

Cash like that didn't drop into his hands too often. And he hadn't even had to steal it.

Of course he hadn't quite carried off his part of the bargain, but the man who'd paid him would have a hell of a time getting his money back.

All Booker Dell cared about now was that his face was ripped up bad. When it finally healed, there would be ugly freaking scars. That demanded payback.

Too bad, especially since Alexis Beranger was a good-looking bitch. Now he'd have to change that. A bottle of acid in the face the way he'd done with Missy

Evers would mess Alexis up so bad that men would get sick to their stomachs just looking at her.

But first, he'd give her the kind of night she'd never forget. It would be the last time any man would willingly climb in bed with her. Booker Dell was not without a twinge of compassion.

DRIVING-HOME TRAFFIC HAD been bumper to bumper when Alexis and Tommy had left Dallas. But now that they'd turned off the main highway, they shared the blacktop road with only a spattering of other cars and pickup trucks.

Tague pushed the speed limit on the straight, flat road, flying past rows of trees and miles of barbed wire fences.

Alexis sat in the backseat of the double cab next to Tommy, a package of frozen peas she'd grabbed out of her freezer on her way out pressed against her eye.

"Boo-boo hurt, Mommy?" Tommy reached over to give her a comforting pat.

"I'm okay, sweetheart. It doesn't hurt. It just looks funny."

He'd calmed down now, but he'd become so upset when Tague had started carrying his toys out of the apartment that he'd thrown a nerve-racking and ear-blasting temper tantrum. It had taken a bit of persuasion to convince him that he was going in the truck with his prized possessions. And she'd had to promise him that she'd ride in the seat next to him all the way.

She tried to hand Tommy the last quarter of his peanut butter and jelly sandwich.

"All done, Mommy."

"Almost," she corrected. "You have a few more bites."

He shook his head and made a monotonous noise that sounded like an engine with a dead battery.

"You have to finish the sandwich so you can grow big and strong."

"Want kokalat."

She handed him his sipper cup. "If you drink your milk and finish your sandwich, you can have *one* square of chocolate."

Amazingly, he took a sip of milk and then exchanged the cup for the rest of his sandwich. He nibbled slowly, and her mind went back to the phone call that had chilled her to the bone.

Even now, she was so on edge she couldn't think straight. Her nerves were frazzled to the point of meltdown.

So close to a meltdown, in fact, that she'd almost told Tague everything back at the apartment. Then somehow her sense of survival had checked in and plunged her into reality. No matter how sympathetic Tague appeared, she couldn't trust him or anyone else with the truth.

Far better that he think it was the carjacker who'd made the call.

"All done, Mommy." Tommy held up his hands to show that he had indeed finished his sandwich.

"You ate every bite," she bragged.

He grinned and her chest constricted painfully. She'd broken the law, crossed every line, and taken justice in her own hands. All to keep Tommy safe. She couldn't give into weakness now.

But why the phone call from Scott? If he had her phone number, he must also know that she went by the name of Alexis Beranger now. He'd know exactly where to find her.

She'd lived every day of the last seven months in fear that he'd burst through the door one day and it would all be over. She'd go to jail, and he'd take Tommy home with him.

Tommy would never be safe again. He couldn't fend for himself against his father's demons. He thrived on love. He needed her.

She gave him his square of chocolate. He gobbled it down and then reached for her with his sticky hands. She kissed his fingertips and then cleaned his face and hands with a wet wipe.

Tague turned onto a meandering two-lane asphalt road. After a mile or two, they reached a driveway bordered by ancient oaks and protected by double metal gates. The bronzed sign hanging above the gate told her they'd arrived at Bent Pine Ranch.

Tague touched a control button on his visor and the gates swung open.

Alexis sat up straight, a new kind of nervousness setting in as they clattered over the cattle gap.

She looked around. The setting sun was dead ahead, casting a golden hue over a sea of green—grasses that swayed in the wind, the needles of towering pines, the dark, shiny leaves of a magnolia tree. And in the midst of it all, cattle grazed lazily in fenced pastures.

The pastoral scene embodied a kind of peaceful existence she'd never experienced but desperately needed. But Tague was not just a simple cowboy. She wouldn't be spending the night in a quiet, safe bunkhouse away from prying eyes.

His family was wealthy and socially connected. And they'd report her to the sheriff in a New York minute if they suspected she was anything less than a law abiding citizen.

"Where is the house?" she asked.

"Another quarter mile and over a slight rise."

She was pointing out the cows to Tommy when the Lambert home came into view. It sprawled out in every direction as if it couldn't decide where it should start or finish. The steep brown roof was multigabled with at least three chimneys.

But other than being large, it was nothing like Alexis had expected. Instead of massive doors and a huge circular driveway that screamed wealth and substance, there was a charming porch with rockers and plants and a porch swing loaded with colorful pillows. The driveway was an extension of the road they'd come in on. It led to the side of the house and a separate four-car garage.

The house was wood, painted a pale forest-green so that it fit in with the surroundings as if it had sprung up from the earth the way the towering pines had.

Tague stopped the car near the front door. "I'll take you in and introduce you to the family and then I'll come back for your things."

"Just the small red duffel," she said. "That and the tote I put in the front seat hold everything Tommy and I will need for tonight."

"Then I guess I won't need the forklift," he teased.

By the time Tommy was unbuckled, Tague had rounded the car and opened her door. Tommy crawled out and then reached back for his stuffed bear.

"Teddy like cows."

"Good," Tague said, "because we have plenty of cows and horses, too."

Tommy's face lit up. "Go see the horseys."

"Great idea, little buddy. As soon as we get your luggage inside."

A white-haired woman stepped onto the porch and waved.

A rush of guilt swept though Alexis, adding another layer of complexity to her already burgeoning emotional chaos. She had no right to bring her problems into this family.

But Tommy was already running ahead, excited by the promise of horses.

It was too late to back out now.

Chapter Five

Alexis's first impression of Carolina Lambert was that she was even more stunning in person than she looked in the newspapers. Simply dressed in a long, gored denim skirt and a white blouse, she moved and spoke with a charming grace that Alexis had seldom encountered before.

Carolina's short brown hair curled about her heart-shaped face and her soft amber eyes lit up when she smiled. She had to be in her fifties, but she could have passed for younger had she not had three grown sons.

Aunt Sybil was older, perhaps mid-sixties. There were few wrinkles in her heavily made-up face, but she had fatty jowls that tugged her lips in a permanent expression of disapproval. And the infamous black wig did look a bit like a raven had landed and died on her head.

Grandma Pearl was delightful. Tague clearly had inherited her smile. Tommy took to Pearl instantly, or at least the second she'd found out he'd already eaten and presented him with a homemade peanut butter cookie.

A chocolate square and cookie. He'd be hyped tonight, but after Scott's phone call, a one-night sugar high seemed a minuscule concern.

Within minutes of entering the house, introductions

had been made and they gathered on an air-conditioned back porch that had been glassed in and furnished with comfortable chairs and sofas. Baskets of magazines and books were scattered about the area and the fragrance from a large basket of daisies perfumed the air.

Belle had the seat of honor, a play chair placed so that she was in the middle of all the action. The baby girl was absolutely precious, and Carolina and the rest of her family clearly adored her.

If they were that enamored of a foster child, perhaps it wasn't that unusual for the Lamberts to take in people who needed help. Alexis definitely qualified tonight.

"How about some raspberry iced tea?" Tague's Aunt Sybil asked as she handed Alexis a tall glass wrapped in a napkin to absorb the condensation. "It's perfect for these hot summer evenings. But there's regular iced tea if you'd prefer."

"Raspberry tea sounds delicious," Alexis said truthfully. Her throat was so dry it was practically raspy.

"There's sherry, too," Pearl said, smiling and holding up her etched crystal cordial stem to expose her beverage of choice.

"Grandma's a loyal sherry drinker," Tague said.

"It's good for the body and the soul," Pearl said with a sly wink.

"And here's a regular iced tea for you, Tague," Sybil said as she handed him a glass. "Fresh brewed and strong, just the way you like it."

"Thank you. Real men don't drink raspberries."

"Can I get your son something to drink?" Sybil asked Alexis. "We have milk and orange juice."

"No," Tommy answered for himself as he scooted

closer to Alexis. He'd settled back into his bashful-around-strangers mode now that he had his cookie.

"No, thank you," Alexis corrected him. Tommy ignored the etiquette prompt.

She envied him that he could emotionally pull away and shut out the roomful of strangers. In spite of the warm hospitality that filled the cozy space, she was becoming increasingly nervous. Her secrets seemed less safe by the second. Too many people. Too much friendly chatter.

Far too little anonymity.

They engaged in a few minutes of small talk about the ranch and the weather before Carolina voiced the question they likely all wanted to ask.

"Tague mentioned a carjacking and a car chase. Is that how you injured your eye?"

"I'll explain it later," Tague said. "Not the best time to get into it." He nodded toward Tommy as if to remind them that he was present and didn't need to hear any more talk of the danger.

"I understand," Carolina said. "But perhaps Alexis needs an ice pack for her eye."

"I'll take you up on that later," Alexis said. "I've been treating it with ice for most of the afternoon."

Tague's Adam's apple bobbed as he gulped down half his glass of tea. "I promised to take Tommy out to see the horses. We should probably get on it before dark. Alexis, do you want to come along?"

"I doubt he'd go without me."

Carolina blotted her wet lips on a napkin and turned to Alexis. "Maybe I should see if Blake will drive over and take a look at your eye and that bump on your head."

"Yep," Tague agreed. "Just what Alexis needs, a horse doctor."

"He's a veterinarian whose ranch borders ours," Carolina explained. "He's also a family friend. I'm sure he'll tell you if he thinks you should see a regular M.D."

"I appreciate the offer, but I did see a doctor today," Alexis said. "I really am fine."

"Then by all means, go with Tague and Tommy to the horse barn. I'll show you to your suite when you get back."

"Actually, I'd love the chance to freshen up a bit before I do anything else," Alexis said. "It's been a long and very chaotic day." And she'd do or say most anything to delay a trip to see giant, stamping stallions.

"I'm sure the day was quite stressful, but the worst is over now. I'm really glad Tague brought you to the ranch to spend the night." Carolina smoothed her skirt with the palm of her hand. "Have you two known each other long?"

"Tell you what," Tague said, running interference. "Aunt Sybil, why don't you get the ice pack and show Alexis and Tommy to the guest suite? I'll fill Mother in on all the details before her curiosity spins totally out of control. I already put Alexis's luggage in the room."

Sybil preened as if she'd been granted a prize. "I'd be delighted to assist."

Alexis stood and followed her, grateful to escape the family confab and to at least wash her face and dab some gloss on her lips.

Her appearance had been the least of her worries before they entered the house. Now she was embarrassingly aware that compared to the others, she looked as if she'd been delivered by a trash truck.

Her white shorts were streaked with the dust she'd collected digging clothes from the back of her closet. Worse, she hadn't had time to shower since she'd chased her disappearing Honda through the supermarket parking lot. Perspiration was no doubt embedded in her skin and clothes.

Add the swollen, black eye and the knot on her head that made her hair lopsided, and it was a wonder she hadn't frightened poor Grandma Pearl into a heart attack, or at least sent her running for another glass of sherry.

On the bright side, looking as she did right now, it was incredibly unlikely that anyone in Tague's family would recognize her from her short and lackluster movie career. So all she needed was for Tague's memory to fail him for a few more hours.

Actually, he may not have seen her movies, either. So few had. Perhaps she just reminded him of an old friend.

In the morning, she'd be on the run again. Maybe north this time, to the Canadian border and beyond. Actually, Mexico would make more sense since it was much closer. But the thought of going anywhere hotter than Dallas in July was a major turnoff.

But first things first. Before she crossed any border, she needed a new fake ID. She had no idea how to come by that in Texas.

She was still thinking about escape options when Sybil opened a door and ushered her and Tommy into a charming room that was nearly as spacious as Alexis's entire apartment.

A king-size mahogany four-poster bed was positioned so that it looked out over the countryside through a wide window. The painted shutters were open to let in slanted rays of a sun that was flirting with the horizon. The sun didn't fully set these evenings until somewhere around 8:30.

Two comfy oversize chairs sat near the window. Framed still-life and landscape paintings hung on the walls. A bouquet of fresh-cut flowers filled a crystal vase that rested on one of the bedside tables.

Even the bed covers were pulled back, tempting her to shimmy beneath them.

The bedroom was far less opulent but ten times more inviting than the bedroom she'd shared with Scott in his massive beachfront mansion. Here the focus was on comfort. There, it had all been for show.

Sybil opened a door on the far side of the room to an adjoining bedroom. "This isn't as large or as comfortable as the main guest room, but it's big enough for the boy. And he'll be nearby so you can hear him if he gets up during the night."

Alexis stepped into the room. There were two twin beds with arched iron headboards. Both were covered in beautiful matching quilts, the patterns similar but not exact. A mahogany French sleigh armoire took up most of one wall.

The wall-mounted TV was the only real reminder that they were living in the twenty-first century. That and the air conditioner that had managed to keep the entire house at a comfortable temperature in spite of the record-breaking heat.

"Come see your room, Tommy," Alexis said. He sidled past her for a peek.

"You'll have your own bed and you can watch your videos."

He walked over and ran his finger along the stitching

in one of the quilts. "Blue and yellow," he said, naming the colors.

"Yes. Blue and yellow and some green, too."

He started to climb onto the bed. "Wanna watch TV. Okay, please."

"Okay. I'll see what I can find, but take off your shoes before you get on the bed."

He kicked out of his brown leather sandals and crawled on top of the quilt.

Alexis found a cartoon channel for him and then returned to the larger guest room.

Sybil opened another door. "This is the bathroom for both guest rooms, so you'll have to share with Tommy."

"I'm sure I can handle that." She did it every day.

"I readied the suite for you myself right after Tague called and said you were coming. I put out fresh towels and my special honeysuckle bath oil and soap. I buy it at a gift shop/tea room in Oak Grove. It smells just like the honeysuckle that grows on the fence out by the swimming hole."

"Thanks, Sybil. I'm sure I'll love it." Alexis put the ice pack back against her bruised flesh.

Sybil stepped out of the bathroom. "That's about it. If you need something you don't see, just ask."

"I will, but I can't imagine what it would be."

Sybil stood by the door to the hallway but didn't leave. "It may not be any of my business," she said, "but exactly how did you get that black eye?"

There was no use not telling her, now that Tommy was in the other room and engrossed in a noisy cartoon. If she didn't, Carolina surely would once she got the full scoop from Tague.

But Alexis would go light on details and make her version short and to the point.

"My car was stolen today, carjacked from a supermarket parking lot with Tommy in the backseat. I tried to fight the thief off and he punched me in the face."

Sybil looked horrified. "Oh, my God. Tommy was in the car with a thief. You must have been terrified."

"I was. I'm still shaking inside from the incident."

"Well, at least you had the good sense to fight the man off. What happened then?"

Alexis gave a skimpy synopsis of the chase and the wreck, trying to keep the drama as low-key as possible. The look of horror never left Sybil's face.

"It's incredible that Tague was there for you. I mean, what were the odds he'd show up at the exact moment you needed him?"

"I'm not sure of the odds, but he definitely came through in a crunch."

"You can always count on Tague to do the right thing without thinking of himself."

"I'm finding that out."

"Where's Tommy's father?"

"We're divorced." It was a lie Alexis had told many times over, yet this time it tasted metallic on her tongue. The Lamberts had welcomed her into their home as if she were an old friend and she was betraying that trust.

"I guess he's mighty upset tonight, too, knowing his son could have been badly injured. I'm surprised he didn't rush right over and take you and Tommy with him."

"He doesn't live in the area."

"Then I'm glad Tague brought the two of you out

here tonight. No one should be alone after something like that."

"I tried not to involve Tague," Alexis said. "He insisted I come here for the night, but I'll be leaving first thing in the morning."

Sybil poked the fingers of her right hand into her wig and scratched. The raven moved as if it were about to spring back to life.

"We'd be glad to have you if you decide to stay a few days. And you're in good hands with Tague. He can handle anything that comes his way. All the Lambert men can."

But they'd never run into Scott Jeffery Hayden before. And they wouldn't now. Alexis would see to that.

Once Sybil left, Alexis returned to the second bedroom to check on Tommy. His eyes were heavy and he'd snuggled beneath the quilt. In spite of the sugar overload, she was sure he was down for the count. There would be no visit to the horse barn tonight.

Alexis whispered a heartfelt hallelujah for that.

To make sure he didn't wake and yell to go see the horses, Alexis opted to skip his nightly bath for once. She retrieved a warm, wet cloth from the bathroom and wiped the day's grime from his body. He whimpered and squirmed but didn't fully rouse as she changed him into his pajamas.

"Good night, sweet Tommy," she whispered as she tucked him in and kissed the top of his head.

She tiptoed to the door and then stopped to look back at him. So innocent. So trusting.

I'll never let your father get you back, Tommy. I'll keep you safe no matter what it takes.

Unexpectedly, her eyes filled with tears. She might

be able to keep him from Scott, but at what price? What kind of life could she give Tommy if they had to keep running forever?

TAGUE FINISHED THE explanation and then took an orange from the fruit bowl in the middle of the kitchen table. He peeled it while his mother digested the information.

Replaying the events for her had been a potent reminder of how tragically different the situation could have turned out.

Carolina sat quietly for a few moments and then leaned forward, resting her elbows on the table. "Poor Alexis. It must be difficult enough to raise a child as a single parent without having to deal with something this frightening. I'm glad you were there for her."

"So am I."

"Things happen for a reason. God put you there. There's no other way to explain how you'd be in that exact spot at that exact time. At breakfast, you were still trying to decide if you were going to pick up the saddle today or wait until tomorrow."

"No argument from me," he said.

"How long has Alexis been divorced?"

He swallowed a bite of orange. "Couldn't tell you."

"It can't have been too long. Tommy's barely two. Does she have sole legal custody of him?"

"I don't know that, either."

"A boy needs his father unless there's a very good reason why he shouldn't be in his life."

Like physical abuse. Tague didn't really want to get into that with his mother tonight. Besides, it was up to Alexis to decide how much of her life story she wanted to share with his family. He was fairly sure there were key elements about her problems with her ex that she hadn't shared with him.

He pulled off another orange segment. "I'm sure Alexis is doing what's best for Tommy."

"I am, too, but I'm just surprised she didn't call his father after the carjacking attempt. You'd think she'd have explained more to you. After all, you were with her all day."

"Yes," Tague said, "but it wasn't what you'd call a social affair."

"It was social enough that you invited her and Tommy to stay with us instead of one of her friends. And she accepted. She wouldn't have if she hadn't warmed up to you."

"'Warmed up'? I don't know where you're going with this, but it best not be toward one of your matchmaking schemes. Alexis is here for one night and one night only. It's no big deal."

"I'm not scheming, but Alexis does seem like a very nice young lady. And she's quite attractive."

More than attractive—she was downright hot and she pushed all his buttons. Not only did she incite sexual arousal, she stirred protective instincts so strong they overwhelmed him.

Excellent reasons for him to keep his distance and ignore any misguided attraction. He planned to get married and have kids one day, but that was several years down the line for him.

He had a lot more living to do and dozens more young ladies to two-step around the dance floor before he settled down to one woman and the responsibility of fatherhood.

Carolina shifted in her chair, but didn't get up. "Say

what you will. I'm just glad Alexis and her son are here with us tonight. I want us to do whatever we can to help her."

Tague finished his orange and then leaned back and stretched his legs beneath the kitchen table. "If you're gung ho to help Alexis, she did mention that she needs a job. Maybe you should talk to Durk about finding a spot for her in the company."

"That's an excellent idea, and I'm sure he can," Carolina said. "If nothing else, he always needs temporary workers to replace women going on maternity leave. I'll call him right now." She stood and then abruptly sat back down. "I guess I shouldn't. He's in Saudi Arabia on business."

"On very important business. You can talk to him when he gets back." Not that there was any guarantee Alexis would even be in Texas then, much less in the Dallas area.

"I have an ever better idea," Carolina said.

"It is never a good idea when you get that conspiratorial gleam in your eyes."

"There is nothing conspiratorial about my gleam. It's just the glow of pure genius."

"So let's hear your plan."

"I've been thinking of hiring a personal secretary."

"Since when? That's the first I've heard of it."

"Since I agreed to head up the annual drive to fund the inner city youth programs last month. That with my other charity responsibilities and sitting on the symphony board is very time-consuming. Either I hire help or I have almost no time at all for myself and Belle."

"You do realize how long the daily commute would take Alexis?"

"She won't have to commute. That's the beauty of this arrangement. She and Tommy can live here on the ranch. You said yourself that she only has a small, crowded apartment in the city, so she should be thrilled for the chance to move from there."

As difficult as it had been to get Alexis to agree to spending one night on the ranch, he seriously doubted she'd choose to move out here. But even if the job and living arrangement worked for Alexis, they would not work for him.

Alexis wasn't the kind of woman he could be around every day and ignore. The temptation would be rabid.

"Her moving here is not a good idea, Mother."

"It's not as if I expect her to live in the guest suite."

"The horse barn would be a little smelly."

"Don't be ridiculous, Tague. You can have the old foreman's cabin fixed up for her and Tommy. It's the perfect size. It just needs some paint and new carpet and some of the kitchen appliances replaced."

"It would be easier to build a new cabin than to repair that old place."

"That's an excellent idea. And she won't need child care because she can bring Tommy to work with her. I'm sure he won't be in the way."

Tague pushed back from the table and stood. "Do you hear yourself? You're planning the life of a woman you barely know. And how much help can she really be to you if she's taking care of Tommy? That in itself appears to be pretty much a full-time job to me."

Disappointment tugged at his mother's mouth. "I guess that could be a problem."

"Call Durk, Mother. If she wants to work for him,

she can hire a babysitter just like every other working mother in Dallas."

"It almost sounds as if you're afraid to have her around."

"Yeah. Call me smart. Moving Alexis and Tommy in here would be asking for trouble. Besides, I'm sure she's not interested. How many single women do you know who are just dying to move from the city to a ranch?"

"I suppose you're right."

Damn straight. He definitely didn't need a seductive temptress living in his backyard.

"Now that we have that settled, I'd better go take Tommy out to see the horses. I figure it's near bedtime for him."

Tague walked to the guest suite and tapped on the door.

"Come in." The invitation was low and a bit breathy, almost as if Alexis had been crying.

He opened the door and stepped inside. Alexis was standing next to the window in a pair of soft pink pajamas. Her hair was damp from the shower. The bruise beneath her right eye had deepened to a blend of blue and dark purple. Both her eyes were red and slightly swollen.

His chest constricted painfully and his insides felt as if someone had reached inside him and turned them inside out. Maybe it was just her vulnerability, but it was all he could do not to walk across the room and take her in his arms.

"You don't look as if you're ready to go see the horses," he said.

"Tommy fell asleep. I don't want to wake him."

"That's okay. He can see the horses in the morning."

"I don't think so, Tague. I'd like to leave as early as

possible. I'll call for a taxi so I think we should just say our goodbyes tonight."

His stomach knotted. "Where will you go?"

"I haven't decided, but somewhere far away from Dallas. I'd been thinking about it even before today. The carjacking just provided the impetus. And now that I have most of my belongings out of the apartment, there's really no reason to go back."

So unless he did or said something to change her mind, this would be the final goodbye. His mind said to let her go. His heart and body weren't buying it.

His brains lost the battle.

"Forget about leaving, Alexis. I have a proposition for you that's too good to refuse."

Chapter Six

Alexis was shocked by the offer to work for Carolina Lambert. A day ago she would have jumped for joy at a way to make some much-needed money and not have to leave Tommy with a sitter all day. Now it was a pipe dream. Once again, Scott had twisted her life into an impossible situation.

She brushed her damp hair behind her ears and dropped to one of the upholstered chairs. "Your mother doesn't even know me. Why would she want me to work for her?"

"Snap decisions are not unusual for Mother, especially when it comes to people. She seems to think the two of you would make a good team."

"Did you explain about the kidnapper and that hiring me might be inviting danger to the ranch?"

"I seriously doubt that would affect her decision."

"Why?"

"In the first place she'd consider danger all the more reason for you to stay here. It's extremely unlikely the carjacker would be foolish enough to show up here. We have an alarm system and cameras at the gate."

"Couldn't he avoid the gate and the cameras altogether by just breaking through the fence?"

"He could," Tague agreed. "But then he'd still have me and a dozen wranglers to deal with. The odds would not be in his favor."

That might all be true if it was the carjacker she was worried about. But in spite of what she'd told Tague, the call hadn't been from the carjacker. All the alarms and cameras in Texas wouldn't deter Scott. He'd show up with an army if need be.

No matter how persuasive Tague's argument, no matter how much she'd like to say yes to Carolina's offer, she didn't dare take her up on it.

"It's a lovely offer, Tague. Tell your mother how much I appreciate it. But I have to say no. It's not the best solution for Tommy and me or for her."

"Mother will be disappointed." He stepped closer and rested a hand on her shoulder. "So will I."

His touch triggered a surge of awareness and a swell of regret. There was undeniable chemistry between them, an attraction that shouldn't be there, but persisted anyway.

Given time, they might have shared something great. Now she'd never know.

"I guess I should go and let you get some rest," he said. "But don't bother with the taxi. I'll drive you into town and make certain you're able to rent a vehicle."

"It's not necessary."

"Maybe not, but it's sensible. The better idea might be for me to go with you to a car dealer so that you could go ahead and replace the Honda. I have friends who could give you a great deal."

Naturally, he would. But the offers wouldn't be for anything she could afford. "I'm not quite ready to purchase yet."

"If money's an issue, I could front you the insurance money and you could pay me back when you get their check," he offered.

"Are you even for real, cowboy?"

He tugged her to her feet and pulled her into his arms. "I'm as real as it gets."

She knew he was going to kiss her. Knew she should stop him. Instead she melted into the thrill and the taste of him. Passion claimed her so completely that she literally lost her breath.

When Tague pulled away, she felt a burning in her lungs and a hunger deep inside her that she had little chance of ever satisfying.

Tague walked to the door. "If you change your mind, the job offer still stands."

"I'll think about it."

She'd no doubt think of little else except for the kiss that had just blown her mind. But nothing would change.

She dropped back into the chair as his footsteps receded down the hallway, tucking her feet beside her and pulling a cashmere throw over her legs.

Her fingertips trailed her lips, and she could swear she still felt the heat from his kiss.

At one time she'd been almost as enamored of Scott. Not physically, the way she was with Tague. She'd never felt anything that compelling and sensual for Scott.

But she'd been awed by Scott's reputation and acclaimed genius. Practically every actress and actor in Hollywood had been. Alexis had been so nervous about meeting him the first time she'd auditioned for a role in one of his movies that she'd forgotten her lines.

She was certain she'd blown her big chance. She'd been devastated. But she'd gotten a call back. And then she'd received the coveted invitation to the Hayden Malibu mansion.

What she hadn't realized was that the visit would be an audition, as well.

That time she'd gotten the role. One month later Tommy had been growing inside her.

SCOTT JEFFERY HAYDEN was thoroughly pissed. He's spent two weeks setting this up and then the carjacking had flopped like his latest production was threatening to do. None of it had been his fault.

"I guess I should have come down there and taken care of things myself instead of trusting it to some bungling, inept private detective."

"You called the shots, sir. I did exactly as you directed."

"If you'd done things right, my son and my wife would be on their way back to California."

"Your wife is a hellcat. But we're back on track. She split within an hour after you called her."

"Perfect. Did you go though her apartment as I instructed?"

"Yes, but she didn't leave much behind except the furniture and some overripe bananas."

"Then it appears she's left for good?"

"Looked that way to me. Not a stitch of her clothes left in the apartment. I found some kid's clothing, but it looked like stuff Tommy might have outgrown. Your son's getting big, Mr. Hayden. Looks like a boy now instead of a baby."

"Did you take pictures of the apartment?"

"I did. I followed all your instructions to the letter."

"Then you know where my wife is now?"

"Not exactly."

"Explain that comment."

"She left here with that same man who was with her this morning at the scene of the wreck."

"The cowboy?"

"Yes, sir."

"Don't tell me they rode off into the sunset on a couple of palominos."

"They left in his pickup truck, but he's not just a cowboy. He's one of the richest ranchers in Texas."

"What's his name?"

"Tague Lambert."

So his wife had taken up with a cowboy. That surprised him almost as much as her giving up on Hollywood had. Not that she could act, but she looked great on the big screen. A lot of actresses had made it big on less.

"Locate my ex-wife or heads will roll, starting with yours."

"Yes, sir."

"When you find her, call me. I'll take over from there. It's time to let the dogs out."

When he was through with her, she'd beg to come home. Right up to her dying breath.

NIGHT WAS AT its blackest when Tague roused from a restless sleep. No silvery moon rays angled across his bed, and thunder rumbled like discordant drums. But thunderstorms were common in July and wouldn't explain the vague apprehension that had crept into his subconscious and forced him awake.

He'd been dreaming. Remnants skulked into his consciousness. Alexis had been in the dream. Only she'd had dark hair. She'd been running along the muddy banks of a bayou with alligators nipping at her heels like attack dogs.

He'd tried to catch up with her, but no matter how fast he ran, the distance between them increased.

The dream fragments continued to coalesce. And then the truth slammed into him and Tague knew exactly who Alexis Beranger reminded him of.

She'd been in a movie he'd watched a few weeks ago when he couldn't get to sleep. Most of the movie had been shot in a swamp. The acting was shoddy, the plot convoluted, the ending contrived.

But the female lead had been spellbinding. Beautiful. Seductive. Hypnotic eyes.

Other than their hair, the star and Alexis looked enough alike to be twins.

Wide-awake now, Tague threw his bare legs over the side of the bed, walked to his desk in his boxers and clicked the mouse. The monitor lit up displaying his home page.

Within minutes he'd discovered the name of the starlet from the movie.

Melinda Ryan.

He scrolled the entries quickly, then double-clicked on one that created a knot in the pit of his stomach.

Melinda Ryan, wife of famed movie director Scott Jeffery Hayden, suspected in the disappearance of her eighteen-month-old stepson, Jeffery Thomas Hayden.

The report was dated December 12 of last year. Seven months ago.

Once he started reading, he had a vague recollection of hearing this story mentioned on the nightly news. He'd figured it was just a publicity stunt at the time or an argument between a couple of Hollywood types.

Apparently, it had been much more.

With each new detail, Tague grew more alarmed.

Melinda Ryan Hayden. Age 25.

Actress and fourth wife of Scott Jeffery Hayden.

Suspected of kidnapping her stepson from their Southern California home after setting their home on fire.

Scott Hayden and the servants barely escaped with their lives. Melinda had been previously hospitalized for an emotional breakdown after going after her husband with a saber.

Mr. Hayden had gone on nationwide TV to plead for his wife to come home with the child or at least let him know the baby was safe.

There was no mention that the famed director had ever been reported for abusing anyone.

Tague finished that article and went on to others, interspersing the updates with sites showing photos of Melinda. The pictures spanned her short acting career and her life as the wife of the Scott Jeffery Hayden.

One photo was of Melinda, Scott and his late wife Lena Fox frolicking at the beach behind his Malibu estate. Melinda had her arm around Lena's neck as if they were fast friends. There was another of Melinda and Lena taken mere days before Lena died from an overdose of sleeping medication and antidepressants. Lena looked pale and reed thin. Melinda was holding Tommy.

Tense and trying hard not to jump to the obvious conclusion that he was harboring a fugitive, Tague scrutinized each photo. There was a striking resemblance between Melinda and the woman who called herself Alexis Beranger. But there were notable dissimilarities, too.

Melinda Ryan's hair was coal-black and curly. Alexis's was blond and straight. A little peroxide and a hair-straightening product could have produced that change.

In most—but not all—of the photos, Melinda's lips seemed fuller and more pronounced. Airbrushing or a cosmetic treatment could explain that.

Melinda's eyes were black as onyx. Alexis's were a bluish-orchid. Both were mesmerizing. A pair of contacts could provide instant change in eye color.

A bolt of lightning zigzagged across the room and the electric current blinked off and then back on again. Tague paced the room while the computer rebooted, unplugging it to rely on battery power as the storm intensified.

Nothing he'd seen or read proved that Melinda Ryan and Alexis Beranger were one and the same. But nothing contradicted it, either.

If they were, it explained a lot of things that had made no sense before.

Like Alexis's desire to leave the scene of the wreck today without talking to the cops. Like her concern over exactly how long it would take to identify the fingerprints in her car.

Like the speed with which she'd cleared everything out of her apartment and the fact that she had no intention of hanging around the Dallas area.

But the fear when the carjacker had Tommy and again when she'd gotten that phone call tonight had been real. He'd stake his best branding iron on that.

She loved Tommy, and he wasn't in danger from her—at least not at the moment. But Tague didn't know much about mental illness, and he'd been around Alexis for less than a day. Who was he to say she was harmless?

But he just could not see Alexis setting a house on fire with her husband and her servants inside.

Rain was pelting the window by the time his computer was back up and running. He didn't bother to touch the mouse. He'd read and seen enough. Now it was time for answers from a woman who may have been playing him like a fiddle in a Texas dance band.

She'd have to do some pretty strong convincing to keep him from calling Sheriff Garcia to check out Tague's suspicions.

If Alexis was Melinda Ryan, then she'd go to jail and Tommy would be returned to his father.

Conflicting emotions banged around inside Tague like short-wick firecrackers on the Fourth of July. He pulled on his jeans and started the long walk to the guest suite. This was one discussion that couldn't wait until daybreak.

Lightning created a fireworks show and a clap of thunder rattled the shutters. Tague figured that was only a preview of the explosion about to shake this house.

This time when he reached Alexis's room, he didn't bother to knock. He turned the knob, swung open the door and stepped inside.

In spite of the raging storm, she was fast asleep. Her breathing was soft and rhythmic, her arms hugging a pillow to her chest. Her hair was dry now and it spread over the pillow beneath her head like a golden halo.

His resolve twisted inside him like a gnarled rope. If she was Melinda Ryan, how could she possibly look so beguiling and so damn innocent?

A bolt of lightning lit the room with streaks of neon-like illumination. Alexis jerked awake as the accompanying blast of thunder struck.

When she saw Tague, she jerked to a sitting position and pulled the covers to her neck. "What do you want?" she demanded, as she flicked on the lamp by her bed. "Why are you here?"

"That's exactly what I was about to ask you, Mrs. Scott Jeffery Hayden."

Chapter Seven

Paralyzing dread ripped through Alexis. She struggled for a steadying breath and willed her heart not to pound its way out of her chest.

This was all her fault. She knew not to come here with Tague, knew she couldn't trust anyone. But then Scott had called and the fear had launched her into panic mode.

Now there was only one way out. She had to talk fast and convincingly and give the best performance of her life.

Avoiding eye contact, she absently turned to watch sheets of rain assault the window. "I don't know what you're talking about, Tague, but if that's some new line to get in a woman's bed, it isn't going to work."

"Don't play games with me, Alexis—or would you rather I call you Melinda?"

"Why would I? And keep your voice down or you'll wake Tommy."

Tague padded across the room, his bare feet almost silent on the carpet. He closed Tommy's door quietly and then walked to the foot of her bed.

"I know all about you, Melinda. You might as well be honest with me."

"The truth is that I don't have a clue what you're talking about."

"If I had any doubt about your identity before walking in here, the terror in your eyes when I called you Mrs. Hayden washed it away."

"Of course I was terrified. I woke up and you were standing over me like some sick voyeur. It's a wonder I didn't scream."

"Look at me when you talk, Melinda. And either stop with the lies or I call the local sheriff now."

He wasn't bluffing. Her options shrank to none, except to try to make Tague believe her.

She finally met his penetrating gaze. "How much do you know?"

"What I read on the internet. That you set your house on fire with your husband in it and then took off with Tommy in the middle of the night."

"I didn't set the house on fire. Scott did. I was the one who was supposed to die. And then he would have made it look like an accident. Since I didn't die, he blamed it on me. And for the record, Melinda is not my real name. I took it when I became an actress. So let's just stick with Alexis."

"Is that your real name?"

"No, but it's grown on me."

"Okay, Alexis, why would your husband try to kill you?"

"Because when I threatened divorce, he flew into one of his barbaric rages. No one rejects Scott Hayden."

"If that's true, why didn't you go to the police and tell them what happened?"

"If you think they would have bothered to even hear

me out before throwing me in jail, you have a lot to learn about Hollywood justice, Tague Lambert."

"Every cop in Hollywood can't be crooked."

"No, but every cop in Hollywood has heard of Scott Jeffery Hayden. He's pure genius in the world of directing. His last five films have topped box-office revenues for weeks on end. He's a legend. I'm the sick wife. The details of my mental and emotional breakdown were covered in all the blogs and gossip tabloids. So why would they believe anything I had to say?"

"I'm not big into the tabloids. Did you have a mental breakdown?"

"No, I was perfectly sane when I tried to kill Scott."

"Murder doesn't sound particularly sane."

"How about self-defense and saving Tommy from an egocentric monster?"

Tague walked to the side of the bed and wrapped his hand around the heavy wooden poster of the headboard. "What happened?"

"It was two months before I fled the burning house with Tommy. It was late, nearing midnight, but Tommy was sick and wouldn't stop crying so I was walking him to try and calm him."

"Where was Scott?"

"I'm getting to that. I knew he wasn't in bed, but I figured he was in his first-floor study working or else taking a midnight walk on the beach as he was prone to do when he was frustrated with a project."

"Did he know Tommy was sick?"

"I'd told him. I doubt it registered. He had little to do with Tommy except when cameras were rolling."

"Go on."

"Our bedroom and the nursery were on the second

floor, but that night I climbed the stairs to the third floor. All of a sudden Scott came rushing from one of the guest rooms. I knew he was furious and high on drugs. I backed away from him, but he just kept coming."

"Was he alone?"

"Yes. He shoved me against the wall and then grabbed Tommy from my arms. The next thing I knew he was dangling Tommy over the balcony and screaming at him to shut up."

Alexis shivered as the memories sent icy fingers crawling up her spine.

Tague sat down beside her. "My God, Alexis. No wonder you tried to kill him."

"I begged him to hand Tommy back to me, but he wouldn't listen." Her voice shook and she wrapped her arms tight across her chest. "I snatched the antique saber from the wall at the landing. I told him I'd gut him like a pig if he didn't hand Tommy back to me. He laughed—and took one hand off Tommy's kicking, squirming body.

"I fell to my knees and begged. Finally, he shoved Tommy into my arms and stormed away. I threw the saber at him as hard as I could. It hit him in the arm, but he was so high and enraged he didn't even know it had hit him. At least not then."

She broke out in a cold sweat. "I'm not crazy, Tague. But I knew that night that I'd either have to escape or I'd end up killing Scott. The next day I asked him for a divorce. That's when he told the police and the psychologists that I'd tried to kill him for no reason."

"And you were hospitalized with a nervous breakdown?"

"Yes, though the private sanatorium where I was

placed was more of a spa with the doors locked than a true hospital. But I was nuts during my confinement, crazy with fear that Scott would fly into one of his rages again and kill Tommy."

"How long were you there?"

"Six weeks."

"And how long were you home before he set the house on fire?"

"One week. Looking back, I'm sure that was the plan when he came to the hospital to pick me up playing the role of loving husband."

"And you escaped the burning house with Tommy and ran."

"It's all I knew to do. But I don't expect you to believe me, Tague. Why should you when no one else does?"

"Right now, I honestly don't know what to believe," Tague said. "If what you're saying is true, there must be a way to get help for your husband and keep you from being arrested for trying to save yourself and Tommy."

"There's only one way to keep Tommy safe, Tague. Let us leave here tonight. Please, just let me go. Do it for Tommy if not for me. If you have a conscience at all, you won't return my son to that monster."

"You mean your stepson, don't you?"

"Yes." But he was hers in every way that mattered.

Tague sat down on the edge of the bed. "I can't let you just walk out of here, Alexis."

Tears burned at the backs of her eyelids. "Please, Tague. Just pretend you never met me. Would that be so hard to do?"

"It would be impossible. Besides, what kind of life can you have if you're always on the run, always pretending to be someone you're not? You'll constantly be looking over your shoulder to see if Scott is closing in on you. That's no way for you or Tommy to live."

"It's a million times better than the alternative."

"Not necessarily."

"I'm wanted for kidnapping. I'll go straight to jail. Tommy will go to Scott. If you turn me in, nothing you can do will change that."

"If you're telling me the truth, I can prove it. Give me a week, Alexis."

"A week of what? Waiting for Detective Hampton to identify and arrest me? Waiting for Scott to show up and kill me before he takes Tommy home with him?"

"A week to investigate the situation. If your husband is the man you describe, you can't be the only one who's experienced his rages. There has to be evidence out there to prove your case against him."

"I don't have a week."

"You will if I keep you safe and out of jail."

"How would you accomplish that?"

Tague raked his fingers through his hair. "I don't know yet, but I'll think of a way. I just need time to explore my options. Will you agree to that week?"

"Do I have a choice, other than sitting here while you call the sheriff?"

"No."

"Then I agree. What do we tell your family?"

"As little as possible. Now we should both try to get some sleep. I'll need my mind crystal clear tomorrow. We'll talk again after daybreak."

"Fine." Unless she got a chance to make a break for it before that.

"By the way, just in case you have any ideas about

sneaking out of the house, I'll be spending the rest of the night in here," Tague said.

So he was a mind reader, too. "How is this going to work if you don't trust me?"

"*My* way."

She still had a say about one thing. She tossed him a pillow. "There's an empty bed in Tommy's room."

"Later, maybe. Right now I'll just settle for a chair."

She lay back down, flicked off the light and stared at the ceiling. She needed to put what had just transpired into some kind of perspective. All she could come up with was that she was being forced to put her trust in the rugged cowboy with the boyish charm and the determination of a mad bull.

Him against Scott Jeffery Hayden.

Heaven help them all.

"HAVE YOU LOST your mind?"

That was exactly the response Tague had expected from his brother Durk. He would have probably said the same after hearing the bizarre tale Tague had just related.

But Tague would be playing an unfamiliar game in a strange milieu. He needed someone he could count on to bounce ideas off of, and there was no one whose opinion he trusted more than Durk.

Tague moved the phone to his left hand so that he could make notes with the right one. "Call me crazy, but I have a hunch Alexis is telling the truth."

"By Alexis, you mean Melinda Ryan?"

"Turns out Melinda is an alias, too. Her Hollywood pseudonym."

"I wouldn't call you crazy, Tague," Durk said. "But

naive might fit. The woman's an actress, remember? She's used to performing. Playing the role of innocent woman can't be that difficult for her."

"I saw one of her movies. Believe me, she's not that good of an actress."

"Then maybe she should be a writer. She has a damn good imagination. Or else she's mentally unbalanced, just as her husband claimed. In either case, you are now harboring a fugitive. That can ensure you reservations at one of our beautiful, fun-filled Texas prisons."

"I realize that. But what if she's telling the truth? Then turning them in to the law might mean sending an innocent woman to prison and a two-year-old kid back to an abusive father."

"I admit that's a tough call."

"You got that right. Still, I guess I shouldn't have brought you into this. No need for both of us to commit a felony."

"Of course you should have called me. We're brothers. The good thing is we can afford a bulldog of a defense attorney to keep us out of prison if it comes to that. So what's your plan?"

"To harbor the fugitive and her son while I investigate her story and try to prove that the legendary Scott Hayden is really Jekyll and Hyde?"

"Hard to believe he could be so successful and still able to hide that kind of character flaw."

"Stranger things have happened," Tague reminded him. "Remember that wealthy Texas woman a few years back who volunteered in nursing homes for years, even won humanitarian awards for her service? Then when she died in a car wreck, they found her own mother starving to death and chained to her bed in the back room of the woman's house."

"That's one of the extreme cases. But you're right. People have been known to hide a multitude of sins even from those who are close to them."

"And that's especially true with people who have money or influence," Tague said. "Scott Jeffery Hayden has both. But he can't have fooled everyone. There must be a few people who've seen his dark side."

"And you plan to find them and make them tell all."

"I plan to give it a shot. That's where you come in."

"The finding them or the torturing them into testifying?"

"Let's start with finding them. I figure I'll need some of the best private investigators in the business. You know more about that kind of thing than I do."

"That's what running a big company will do for you. If I were you, the first person I'd call is Meghan Sinclair."

"A woman?"

"All woman, and she uses that to her advantage whenever needed."

"Has she done work for you before?"

"No, she's not into corporate cases."

"Then how do you know her?"

"I never kiss and tell."

"Nuff said. How do I reach her?"

"I'll email you her contact info as soon as we hang up."

"Any other investigators that you'd recommend?

"Jackson Phelps. He's retired NCIS. Nothing gets past him. He has done some work for us and did a bang-up job. I'll pass his contact information along to you, as well. You might want to wait until you've talked to them before you pursue anyone else. They'll have their own ideas for how best to get this done."

"Good idea. Now all I have to do is decide what to do with Alexis and Tommy. I want to keep Mother, Aunt Sybil and Grandma out of this, so that rules out letting them stay here."

"Not to mention that Detective Hampton will no doubt pay you a visit when he identifies Alexis from her fingerprints and finds out she's missing."

"I'm sure I'll be first on his list."

"Have you thought about Galveston?" Durk asked. "I'm sure you could find a condo to rent somewhere on the beach. That would at least get her out of Dallas."

"I'd rather find her a house somewhere isolated enough that she can take Tommy outside without the risk of anyone seeing them. I figure Hampton will put out an APB on her as soon as he realizes he's let a wanted woman slip his grasp."

"What about Dad's old fishing cabin on Lake Livingston? That's isolated."

"And probably full of spiders. Maybe even snakes. I don't think anyone's used it since Dad bought that golf and fishing condo on Toledo Bend."

"Which we should find time to use more often," Durk said. "But it's not isolated. So that leaves…"

"The hunting camp." The solution came out in stereo, both having thought of it at the same instant.

"It's perfect," Tague said. "Clean. Roomy. And isolated. I'll give the caretakers a week's paid vacation."

"Of course, the fugitive might be afraid to stay out there by herself. When those coyotes howl and the owls hoot, it can get a little spooky."

"She won't ever be there without me."

"You plan to be with her every second?"

"That's the current plan."

"Cozy."

"I can't very well conduct an investigation without her input."

"Just be careful you don't go falling for her. She's a married woman and a wanted criminal."

"Right. I plan to keep my head on straight and my pants zipped."

"I'm looking at Melinda Ryan's picture on the computer right now, bro. Unless you've become a eunuch since I've seen you last, I'd say you've got your work cut out for you."

"I'm up to the task."

"Good. But all kidding aside, be careful. This could spin out of control faster than you can hog-tie a crippled calf and whistle 'Yellow Rose of Texas.'"

"Check." He'd be careful. He just prayed his hunches were right.

And that he had time for lots of cold showers. He had the feeling he was going to need them, regardless of what he'd promised Durk.

"I'm LOOKING FORWARD to working with you too, Meghan. If you're half as good as Durk claims, I'm sure we'll find what we're looking for."

"Just promise me you won't kill the messenger if you don't like my findings."

"I'm just after the truth."

"That's what they all say—until they get it."

"I don't have a dog in the show. I'm just looking to protect the innocent—whoever that might be."

Tague finished the call and jotted down a few last notes. So far, so good. He and Alexis had come up with a plan for what they'd tell his family. And Meghan Sinclair was on board. He hadn't been able to connect with Jackson Phelps yet, but he'd left him a message.

Now he just had to make it through breakfast with the family. He pocketed his phone, dropped the notebook into the top of his duffel and zipped it. He was ready to roll.

He smelled the bacon and heard the chatter and laughter long before he reached the kitchen. Family. There were times he could use a little less of them, but he couldn't imagine life without them. He knew they'd always be there for him.

The way Durk had come through for him this morning even though he had serious doubts about Tague's involvement with Alexis. The way his mother had welcomed Alexis when all she knew about her was that she was with Tague.

He took his family and life on the ranch for granted, too often forgetting that it wasn't that way for everyone. Alexis hadn't mentioned family at all, except for the husband who'd tried to kill her.

Had she abandoned parents and perhaps siblings somewhere down the line, or had they abandoned her?

And if so, why?

He suspected the answer to that would go a long way in explaining why she'd fallen into a relationship with a man like Scott Hayden.

He pushed thoughts of her past life aside as he entered the kitchen. He had enough on his plate without going there.

His mother pressed a cup of coffee into his hand.

"Good morning, and it's time you joined us. We were about to start without you, or at least Grandma was."

Tague spotted Alexis at the table with Belle in her arms. She was occupied with spooning runny food into Belle's mouth and then catching it with the spoon as Belle playfully pushed it out with her tongue.

Her eye wasn't quite as swollen as it had been last night, but the bruises were even more pronounced. The lump on her head, however, was practically undetectable beneath her slightly disheveled hair.

"I see Mother put you to work," he said.

"I can't cook, so I was assigned the one thing I can do. Shovel food into kids."

"She volunteered," Carolina assured him.

"I told her she had to work for her food," he said, making a conscious stab at the light mood that usually came naturally for him.

"Right," Alexis said. "I was afraid he'd make me milk cows."

"We grow beef cattle," he said. "You'd have been milking a long time."

Pearl plopped a lump of butter inside a flaky biscuit. "Look in the refrigerator and get a jar of those plum preserves your Momma just made, Tague."

"The preserves are already on the table," Sybil said. "And it wouldn't hurt you to wait until we've said grace."

"Plate of what?"

"Wait for grace," Sybil repeated as she placed the preserves within Pearl's easy reach.

Carolina carried a platter of bacon and scrambled eggs to the table and set them next to the basket of hot biscuits. Then she returned with Tommy's sipper cup.

"Why don't you sit here next to Grandma Pearl,

Tommy?" Carolina said. "Your mother can sit next to you." She placed the cup of milk by Tommy's plate.

"Wanna go see horseys."

"Next time," Alexis said.

"Not next time. Today time."

"You're right, buddy," Tague said. "A promise is a promise. Eat your breakfast and then we'll go see the horses."

"I think Belle's had her fill," Carolina said. "Why don't we all sit down and say grace and then I'll put her in her play chair?"

Alexis wiped Belle's hands and face with a damp cloth and then kissed the top of her head. Tague watched, amazed that Alexis fit so well into this life when her previous one had been so different.

From a Malibu mansion filled with Hollywood players to a ranch in Texas filled with Lamberts. Either she was a better actress than he'd given her credit for or she had a depth to her he hadn't expected.

When she sat, he took the seat across from hers. Conversation pretty much ceased until Grandma Pearl had finished her speed version of grace and everyone's plates were full.

"This is so good," Alexis said, forking another bite of egg. "Do you always have a huge breakfast like this?"

"Most of the time, except on Sunday," Carolina said. "Then we eat light so that we can make Sunday school on time."

"It's not time for Sunday school," Pearl said. "It's Wednesday."

"It's Tuesday," Sybil corrected.

"I know it's not Sunday," Pearl said.

Sybil reached for the preserves. "You really should wear your hearing aids."

"I don't need them to know what day it is."

"Usually Damien and Tague have been up and working for a couple of hours before breakfast," Carolina said, no doubt to change the subject. "They've normally worked up quite an appetite by now."

"Right," Tague teased, flexing his muscles. "Ordering those wranglers around takes a lot out of a man."

"Don't let him kid you," Carolina said. "He and Damien are both hard workers, just like their father was."

"I believe it. He was great help to me yesterday. And I can't thank you enough for your hospitality. I can't remember when I've felt more at home."

"You're welcome to stay as long as you like. In fact, I'd love it if you stayed for a few more days."

"Thank you, but I've contacted a friend in Tulsa, and she's expecting me. I haven't seen her in awhile so it will be a good chance for us to visit."

"I just hope that carjacker is arrested soon," Sybil said. "No one should be afraid that some brute with a gun will break into her apartment."

"I'm just taking extra precautions," she said. "No one is going to hurt us. Tommy and I are just fine."

Fortunately, Sybil got the message and dropped the subject. Tommy might not understand everything, but yesterday had been traumatic for him. He didn't need reminders.

"You should at least stay long enough for Tague to show you around the ranch," Sybil said. "You could ride the horses down to the swimming hole and cool off after that."

"Maybe some other time," Alexis said. "I have a long

drive in front of me and I know Tague does as well. So as soon as we make a quick trip to see the horses, he can drop me off at the car rental agency."

Carolina turned to Tague. "I didn't know you had a trip planned."

Alexis was playing this to perfection, following their mostly impromptu script with precision. He hoped he did as well.

"I'm driving out to an auction in Colorado. The Calloway ranch's Angus stock is going on the block. I know I told you about it."

"You mentioned an auction in Colorado. I thought you said it was in August. I was considering going with you and spending some time in Vale to escape this heat."

"They moved it up a month, but you should still consider a mountain vacation. I'm sure you could get a friend or two to go with you."

"I may, once Damien and Emma get home. But I'll fly, not drive. You should fly, too. It would save you a lot of time."

"And cause me a lot of hassle. Besides, this way I can stop off in Lubbock and spend some time with my buddy Jack. I haven't seen him since he left the rodeo circuit."

"That's a good idea."

The groundwork was laid. Now there was nothing to do but visit the horses, drive to the hunting camp and kick the investigation into high gear.

His phone vibrated. He pulled it from his pocket and checked the caller ID. Meghan Sinclair.

He excused himself and took the call. "Don't tell me you already have results to report."

"Actually, I have," Meghan said, "but I don't think

it's what you were hoping for. In fact, you might consider it a game changer."

The fun had started. "That didn't take long. Hit me with it."

Chapter Eight

"Melinda Ryan, or Alexis Beranger, as you know her, is considered a suspect in the murder of Lena Fox Hayden."

Murder, and not just attempted murder this time. Tague felt like he was sinking in quicksand. He hadn't anticipated instant gratification, but he hadn't expected this kind of setback, either.

"Let me be sure I have this straight," he said. "Lena Fox was Scott Hayden's third wife, right?"

"Yes, and the mother of the boy Alexis kidnapped."

"I read that Lena had committed suicide."

"Originally the death was ruled a suicide, but there's new evidence to indicate she was murdered."

"How would you get new evidence at this late date? The autopsy must have been conducted over a year ago, long before Alexis and Scott were married."

"Lena died twenty-four months ago almost to the day, when her son was only a month old. Everyone attributed the suicide to severe postpartum depression."

"How long after that did Alexis and Scott get married?"

"Two months."

"The guy certainly wasted no time on grief," Tague said.

"And Alexis wasted no time nabbing the rich widower," Meghan said, keeping it all in disturbing perspective. "Listen, I don't have all the facts yet, but as soon as I have them confirmed, I'll get back to you, if you want me to continue with the investigation."

"Absolutely." But his confidence in Alexis had taken a serious nosedive. "Find out everything you can. See what part Scott Hayden had to play, and if he's been involved with any other women since Alexis left him."

"I can't promise the news will get any better."

"You sound as if you're already convinced Alexis is guilty."

"Not necessarily," Meghan said. "But where there's smoke, there are usually at least a few flames. Alexis is all but smothered in smoke. Nonetheless, I reserve judgment until we have all the facts."

"What's our next move?" Tague asked.

"I'm flying to California tomorrow. I want to talk to the renowned director in person."

"He may not be easy to get to."

"How hard can it be to get his attention? I'm a woman and he's a man."

"Then it's up to you. By the way, how do you know my brother Durk?"

"You should probably ask your brother that question."

Tague planned to do just that the first time he saw Durk in private. But right now he had a two-year-old waiting to see the horseys and a suspected killer waiting to put her life in his hands.

The next few days promised to be anything but dull.

KEEPING PACE WITH a two-year-old tramping through the mud was a refined talent, Tague decided as he tried to get

Tommy from the house to the horse barn. Had Tommy not been so cute, the task would have been downright frustrating.

As it was, watching his antics eased some of the tension Meghan's phone call had produced.

Alexis had wisely pulled bright red galoshes onto Tommy's feet. Good thinking since Tommy seldom stayed on the stone pathway specifically designed for poststorm treks.

The mud was too tempting. He'd run a few feet on the path and then veer off to chase a butterfly or a dragonfly. To her credit, Alexis let him be a boy. Might as well. There was no way he could go anywhere after this without having a bath and changing clothes anyway.

Tommy stopped when he spotted a nice, gooey patch of mud. He looked back at Alexis, flashed a mischievous grin and then jumped in with both feet. Alexis backed up just in time to keep from being splattered.

"How do you ever get anywhere?" Tague asked as Tommy meandered off in a zigzag pattern in pursuit of a tiny frog.

"If I'm in a hurry, I make him ride in his stroller or I pull him in his red wagon—both of which are in the back of your truck. If we're in the park, we mostly follow his pace. However, he's never had this much open space and mud to explore."

"No wonder he's mud happy. There will be plenty of wide open spaces at the hunting camp."

"I can carry him now if we're in a hurry," Alexis said. "But you'd have to carry those muddy boots. I'm not getting them anywhere near me."

"We're not in a hurry. I figure we have at least until tomorrow before Detective Hampton starts trying to track you down. Besides, the boy probably needs a chance to run and play before we buckle him into his booster seat and make him sit for hours."

"How long is the drive to the camp?"

"About three hours. But we'll have to stop for food and supplies. There's game in the camp freezer and staples in the pantry, but nothing in the way of fresh milk, eggs or produce. We'll carry a cooler of beef with us. And, of course, you can get whatever Tommy needs in the way of nourishment."

"Currently that's milk and peanut butter and jelly sandwiches. He tends to limit his menu fare to one dish at a time. But he'll include apple slices on the promise of a chocolate reward."

"Wait until he tastes my French fries."

She narrowed her eyes. "Wow. That's a healthy alternative. Now if you impress him with broccoli that would be true culinary talent."

Tommy splashed his way back to the path. "Where horseys?"

"In that red barn," Tague said, pointing in front of them.

"You'll have to hold on to mine or Mr. Lambert's hand all the time we're around the horses, Tommy. They are big—very, very big. And they're real, not painted plastic like the ones on the park carousel."

Tague scowled. "Carousel ponies? That's like comparing an anthill to a mountain."

"That's the only kind of horse he's been around."

"Then he's in for a real treat if you don't scare him out of it."

"I don't want him to get hurt."

"Stop fretting. I won't let anything bad happen to

him." At least not in the horse barn. Her real worry should be the fact that she'd lose Tommy forever if she went to jail for killing his mother.

The discussion about her being a suspect in Lena's death would have to come sometime today, but not in Tommy's presence.

"This is it," Tague announced seconds later when they reached the horse barn. A few welcoming neighs and some tapping of hooves greeted his voice.

"We have to clean the mud off our boots before we go inside," Tague said as he dragged his right foot across the bristled boot brush. "We don't want big clumps of mud in the straw. It might make someone slip and fall."

Mostly he didn't want the mud on his jeans when he picked Tommy up so that he could see above the stall doors.

Tommy followed suit, though he needed Tague's steadying hand on his shoulder while he dragged each foot through the bristles several times.

Tague finally reached down and swooped Tommy into his arms. The boy stiffened as if he were about to protest. But the second they stepped into the barn, he became too excited to complain.

Carolina's favorite mount snorted and pawed the ground a few times, swinging her dark gray mane for attention.

"Horsey loud," Tommy said.

"That's because she's glad to see us. Her name is Silver. She likes apples and ear scratches." Tague reached over and scratched the horse's ear.

Tommy gingerly put his fingertips to Silver's ear. "Me like apples, too."

"So do I." Tague looked around for Alexis. She was

nowhere in sight. For a second, he thought she'd made a run for it, leaving Tommy behind. Panic hit swiftly. He was already stretching his kid-tending abilities to the limit.

Finally he spotted her, peeking from around the support post.

"Don't tell me you're afraid of horses," he said.

"Of course not. I'm a…I'm a…I'm allergic to them, you know the hair and the hay and the smell."

"You're not allergic. Admit it, you're scared."

"I'm not scared. I just don't see any reason to get so close. I can see them fine from here." She adjusted her sunglasses and produced a fake smile.

It was all he could do to keep from laughing at the spunky fugitive cowering in the shadows. "Come inside," he said. "I promise the horses won't hurt you."

"Won't hurt you, Mommy," Tommy echoed. "'M'on in."

She stepped in cautiously. The smile left his face as the incongruities of the moment and perhaps of their relationship became crystal clear.

She was afraid of horses yet she'd fought a thug twice her size to protect the boy whose mother she was accused of killing. She'd clearly been running scared for months, yet she found a way to make a home for Tommy where he could feel safe.

The only reason she was still here on the Bent Pine Ranch was because Tague had forced her to stay. Yet she fit in like one of the family.

No wonder he couldn't picture how this gorgeous, spunky, indomitable young mother was the same person as the mentally unbalanced, heartless and dangerous Melinda Ryan.

The best he could do was to try his damned best to keep an open mind.

Alexis sidled up next to him. Her scent held the freshness of a summer rain. He fought the impulse to put his arm around her and pull her closer still.

Okay, he'd have to downgrade keeping an open mind to the number two slot on his priority checklist. Number one was keeping his libido under control.

"Have you ever ridden a horse?" he asked.

"Almost. Sort of."

"How can you sort of ride a horse?"

"I sat in a saddle once."

"Was the saddle even on a horse?"

"It was near one."

"That doesn't count. Why were you in a saddle without a horse?"

"It was for a movie," she admitted. "They thought I was an experienced rider so they just brought this horse to where we were shooting a scene and told me to get on."

"But you didn't?"

"I tried. The second I approached the giant animal, he rose up on two legs like he was readying for battle. I backed up so fast I tripped over the electrical cords for the lighting. I destroyed the medieval costume I'd just been cavorting in with the rogue duke of somewhere."

"That must have made an impression."

"Exactly. The director was furious. I had to beg to keep the role. Another mistake on my part. The film was never seen except on TV and then only by insomniacs. My cut amounted to almost enough to buy a hamburger and fries."

"Why did they think you were an experienced rider?"

"I may have mentioned that in my résumé."

"Then you deserved what you got." Tague started back toward the tack room. "Guess I'll have to make an honest woman of you."

"I'm not getting on a horse, Tague. I'm not."

"You'll feel better once you conquer your fears."

"I like my fears the way they are."

"There's nothing to it, Alexis. I'll help you mount Silver. She's as gentle as a lapdog and then you and Tommy can ride around the corral. I'll hold the reins and lead. You'll get the feel of it in no time."

She shook her head. "Don't push your luck, cowboy."

"Wanna ride, Mommy," Tommy chimed in. "Wanna ride Silver."

"You don't want to disappoint the boy," Tague said.

Tommy wiggled to get down from Tague's arms. Tague eased him down and Tommy immediately dived into a pile of fresh straw a few feet away. Tague put a thumb under Alexis's chin and tilted her face until their gazes locked. "Do you trust me to do what I say?"

She closed her eyes for a second and then exhaled slowly. "This isn't about riding Silver anymore, is it?"

"Not at the moment."

"I don't have a lot of choice, do I? I do what you say, or you call the authorities."

"That's not going to cut it, Alexis, not if you really want to prove your innocence. We're not in Hollywood and this isn't a world of make-believe and illusions."

"I know where I am, Tague."

"I'm willing to use every resource I have to help you, but I need you to be totally honest with me about everything. You have to trust me enough to hold nothing back."

"I don't have a lot of experience with trust, Tague. In fact, I don't have any."

"Then we'll just be spinning our wheels for the next week." He leaned in close and put his mouth to her ear so that he could keep his voice to a husky whisper. "Tommy will be the real loser. Is that what you want?"

"No. You know it's not."

"Then trust me. I have no ulterior motives. I have nothing to gain except the knowledge that I've done what I can to make sure you get a fair shake and Tommy stays safe."

"I want to believe you."

"Then do. Trust me."

"I'll try. It's been so long, I don't even know where to start or how to begin letting down the barriers."

"Then let's start with a horse ride. Put yourself in my hands and trust me to keep you safe. Then we'll work from there."

For a second he seriously doubted she could. Then she gave a little salute and relented.

"Okay, Tague. I'll do my best to give this trust thing a shot. I'll get back in the saddle again."

"Atta girl. This time, we'll try it with a horse."

ALEXIS COULDN'T DENY a bit of nerve-tamped elation as they walked back toward the house. Tague had led her and Tommy around the corral not once but three times. Tommy had been ecstatic, especially after Tague had taught him to yell *yee-haw.* She figured he'd be doing it the rest of the day.

Tague was incredible. She wanted desperately to trust him, yet the niggling fear and mistrust she'd harbored for years refused to completely disappear.

The stakes were too high. Tague could change his mind at any second, decide she was guilty and use anything she'd said against her. He lived in world of black and white, a Camelot of sorts where truth was might.

The past three years of her life had been painted in shades of gray and the lines between right and wrong had blurred to the point she could no longer distinguish between them.

She'd never meant to hurt anyone. In spite of that, she'd unknowingly helped destroy Lena and she'd stolen Tommy and became a fugitive.

Tommy ran ahead of them, stopping to splash at every opportunity, though the puddles were quickly drying up. The bright morning sun was a glaring reminder that the temperature might reach a hundred degrees by afternoon.

"I'll have to carry Tommy directly to the bathtub," she said. "Your mother will kill me if he drags that mud into her house."

"There's a hose in the backyard. Wash him off outside."

"He'll love that."

"I think he's got a little cowboy in him," Tague said. "He's taking to ranch life like a wrangler in training."

"No doubt about it," Alexis agreed. "You won him over the second you lifted him atop Silver. He'll drive me nuts begging to come back to the Bent Pine."

But she found it difficult to believe they ever would. No matter how much Tague talked about trust, her best opportunity to stay out of jail and keep Tommy was to go on the run again. Somehow she had to find a way to make him see that.

In order to do that, she needed to find out everything about him she could.

"What was it like growing up on the ranch?" she asked as they neared the house.

"The dream life, though, of course, I didn't realize it at the time. Looking back, I appreciate how lucky my brothers and I were. We had horses and four-wheelers and acres to explore. We were surrounded by friends and family and lived in a house that echoed with love."

"It sounds heavenly." And far more like a dream than any reality she'd ever known.

"Don't get me wrong. It wasn't all fun and games. We had chores to do. And not nearly as many fancy toys as our friends. Dad wasn't keen on kids watching TV or playing video games. He figured a bike, a baseball, a football and a swimming hole should be enough to keep a kid busy."

"He sounds like a man who had it all together."

"I'm not sure anyone ever has it all together, but Dad was a man who put morals and ethics above money, and trustworthiness above popularity. He truly was as good as his word in the oil business and in ranching."

"Was he a good father as well?"

"He was strict, but he knew how to have fun. We still have the tire swing he hung for us. And the tree house he helped us build out of scrap lumber is still standing, though a woodpecker left the roof full of holes."

"Did you and your brothers go to private schools?"

"Nope. Mother is big on community. If she wasn't happy with something about the neighborhood school, she jumped in and did what she could to change it, but never without the involvement of others. She's convinced that it's the sharing that makes everyone feel part of the community. She's a remarkable woman, another thing I didn't fully appreciate until recently."

"She's very gracious."

"And there's not a snobbish bone in her body. To tell you the truth, I didn't even know we were rich until I was in high school."

"You're kidding?"

"No. When I was in the tenth grade, I read an article about the success of Lambert Inc. and I thought, 'Hey, that's us.' I immediately went to my father and told him that since we were rich I should be driving a Corvette to school."

"Did you get one?"

"Hardly. He informed me *he* was rich. I was still living on the dole."

"Did you ever get the Corvette?"

"Not yet. Probably never will. Turns out I'm a pickup truck kind of guy."

"So there are no deep, dark secrets that shaped your life or rattling skeletons hiding in the back of your closet?"

"Afraid not."

"No beautiful woman in a distant European castle waiting for your visit with bated breath?"

"I think you have me mixed up with Prince William or his brother, Harry."

"Impossible. You have a Texas accent. Is there a first love for whom you still pine?"

"Not unless you mean my horse Gabe. He died about four years ago and I still miss him."

Perhaps Tague was as straightforward and as honest as he seemed. Guilt pricked Alexis's conscience. "There's something I need to tell you, Tague."

"I'm listening."

"Remember the phone call that I got just before we left Dallas?"

"The one from the carjacker?"

"Yes, only I lied. It wasn't from the carjacker. The caller was Scott. He didn't say his name. He only said that I knew what he wanted. But I'd know his voice anywhere."

"No wonder you were in such a rush to get out of the house. Why didn't you tell me then?"

"Because I was trying not to get involved with you. If Scott knew my number, I thought he must have known where I lived. I expected him to burst through the door at any second."

"That seems logical," Tague agreed.

"Yes, but the more I think about it, I feel certain he only had my phone number. He may have been trying to trace the call and discover my location. But there is no way he'd have ever just called and given me warning that he was coming if he knew where to find me."

"I want to know if he calls again, Alexis, and don't wait until a day later to tell me."

"No, I won't."

Tommy ran up to show her a bug he'd found under a rock, saving her from any additional talk of Scott. Before she finished examining the bug, she heard Carolina calling for them to hurry.

Alexis took Tommy's hand and pulled him along, albeit a few steps behind Tague.

"What is it?" Tague asked.

"Sheriff Garcia is here to see Alexis. He says it's urgent."

Alexis's heart plunged to her toes. A visit from any sheriff could only mean one thing. She was on her way to jail.

Chapter Nine

Tague had no idea how Garcia had gotten involved in this, but he didn't like it. There was a chance Scott Hayden was behind this visit, but Tague doubted that was the case. Had Scott known Alexis and Tommy were here, cops would be swarming the place. In that situation, Tague would have no choice but to stand back and let them arrest Alexis.

He glanced behind him to see how Alexis was taking the news.

She was leaning over Tommy, holding on to him as if she feared he was about to be plucked away by a vulture. Her face was drawn, her bottom lip sucked between her teeth. The urge to take her in his arms and reassure her was practically devastating.

"Tell Garcia we'll be there in a few minutes," Tague told his mother. "We need to rinse the mud off of Tommy first." At least that would give Alexis a chance to calm down.

"I can do that for you," Carolina offered.

"I'll handle the clean-up job," Tague said, "but you could throw me a bar of soap and a washcloth and towel. I might as well do this right while I'm at it. Besides, there's nothing more refreshing than an outdoor shower in July."

"I can take care of Tommy," Alexis said in a shaky voice. "You can all go inside."

"I'm staying out here with you," Tague said. "Why don't you help Tommy get undressed, Alexis?"

Tommy was already stripping, but as frightened as Alexis looked and sounded, she might do something desperate if he let her out of his sight. Like steal one of the vehicles in the driveway and make a run for it.

He turned on the water and adjusted the nozzle while Alexis pulled the blue knit shirt over Tommy's head. Tague sprayed gently to the backdrop of Tommy's delighted squeals.

Alexis stepped behind him where she could stay dry. "Tell the sheriff I'm not here, Tague," she pleaded, her voice barely a whisper. "Tell him I left while you were working with the horses. Tell him anything. Just get rid of him."

"It's too late for that. He'd know I was lying."

"Then give me the keys to your truck. You can sidetrack him while Tommy and I drive away and then you won't be lying."

"You've run long enough, Alexis. It's time to stand strong and tackle the issues head-on. I'll be beside you all the way."

"Really? Are you going to jail with me? Are you going to take care of Tommy and keep him safe while I'm in front of a judge and jury?"

Carolina returned. She handed Tague the bar of soap and the washcloth and Alexis a big, fluffy towel. "I think the sheriff has good news," she said. "At least he better since he's eaten two pieces of Alda's banana bread and bored me for almost half an hour with talk of his mother's gout."

"Do you know him personally?" Alexis asked.

"Everyone around here knows Garcia," Carolina said. "He's been sheriff for the last twenty years and he was a deputy before that. He's as recognizable around Oak Grove as the bell tower in the Baptist Church."

"And he makes as much noise," Tague said. "I think we're done here. Tommy is squeaky-clean."

"Yee-haw," Tommy called. When Carolina laughed, he did it a couple of more times for her listening pleasure.

"If you'll lay out his clothes, I'll dress him and keep him entertained while you talk to the sheriff," Carolina offered.

"I'd appreciate that," Alexis said. She wrapped the towel around Tommy and Tague threw him over his shoulders and carried him up the stairs and into the house.

"You look like a natural at that," Carolina said.

A witty comeback flew to the tip of Tague's tongue, but he bit it back. He wasn't even sure why except that it didn't seem the time or place to protest that he was a long way from being ready for fatherhood.

He took Alexis's arm as they walked into the parlor where Garcia was waiting.

"Hang in there," he offered as feeble encouragement.

"Please don't mention the word *hang*. I'm about to be sick as it is."

Garcia stood as they entered, dressed in his usual pair of creased khaki pants and a clean khaki shirt. His skin was ruddy and though he was only a few years older than Carolina, his hairline was receding fast.

He put out his hand to Tague. "Good to see you again. Haven't seen hide nor hair of you since the Easter community service. Guess you've been busy."

"A rancher's work is never done," Tague said.

"Same with a lawman. I hear you've been looking around for some more land to buy."

"I'm always in the market for a bargain."

"Reid Olson's thinking of selling off some of his land now that his kids are all married and grown."

"I'll give him a call, but I'm sure that's not what brought you here today."

"No, I'm here to see Alexis Beranger." He put out a hand to Alexis. "You must be the lady in question."

"I'm Alexis Beranger," she said, ignoring his hand.

"That's quite a shiner you got there. Did you get that from the carjacker?"

"I did. How do you know about that?"

"I got a call from Detective Gerald Hampton. He said he's working with you on the case."

"Why would he call you?"

"You're in my jurisdiction, so he asked me to take a ride over here. He didn't know for certain you were at the Lamberts, but he figured you might be, seeing as how he'd run into Tague at your place yesterday."

"So why did Hampton send you out here?"

"He thought Alexis would be happy to learn that her carjacker has been arrested."

"That is good news," Tague said. "Who is he?"

Garcia hitched up his trousers. "Booker Dell Collins. He's bad news. Hampton claims he likes his violence about as well as he likes his crack. And that's plenty."

Alexis put a shaky hand on Tague's arm. "They must have found his fingerprints in my car."

"Not that I know of," Garcia said. "Way I heard it was that someone turned Booker in for the reward money."

"What reward?" Alexis asked.

"Let's sit down and go over this slowly," Tague said. "I'd like to make certain I get the facts straight." He led Alexis to the sofa and then sat down next to her. Garcia sat back down as well, in a chair facing them.

"What's this about a reward?" Tague asked.

"Someone offered a whopping $50,000 reward for information leading to the arrest of the carjacker."

"Who would do that?" Alexis asked. "Certainly no one that I know."

"An anonymous donor."

"That's a lot of money for a carjacking where no one was injured," Tague commented.

"Well, it worked," Garcia said. "A woman who claims to have seen the entire incident from her car called in and identified Booker Dell Collins by name. She said she'd known his mother for years."

"So there was a witness," Tague said.

"Yep, and apparently a credible one. She didn't actually collect the reward yet, but if the arrest sticks, she will. Of course, she opted not to have her identity revealed to the public for fear of reprisal."

"I still can't imagine who'd offer an award of that size," Alexis said.

"Hampton figures it was a business owner whose bottom line is being affected by crimes in that area. It could even be the CEO of the supermarket chain where you were attacked."

It could have been, but Tague had a hunch Scott Hayden was behind this. That amount of money would be nothing to him. But why did he need the carjacker arrested?

Was he trying to protect Alexis? Or did he have a more devious plan? Like not wanting her identified and arrested before he could kill her and silence her claims of rage and attempted murder for good.

"Detective Hampton said to tell you he'd need you to come in and pick the suspect out of a lineup, Mrs. Beranger," Garcia said. "He'll call and let you know when, but he wants you to keep your phone with you so he can reach you. He left you several messages this morning but said you didn't return his calls."

A nod was her only response.

Tague stood to walk the sheriff to the door. "Is that everything?"

"Pretty much." Garcia kept talking, but he'd changed the subject to last night's thunderstorm and the damage lightning had inflicted on a tree in a neighboring rancher's pasture.

Tague's mind had shifted gears as well, but not to the weather. Alexis turned to leave the room before the sheriff was out the door. Tague grabbed her wrist to stop her. This might be the only time they had alone for the rest of the day.

"I need to check on Tommy," she said, once the sheriff was actually gone and the door closed behind him.

"That can wait a minute."

"What now?" she asked.

"What do you know about Lena Fox Hayden's murder?"

Alexis face registered shock. "Lena wasn't murdered. She committed suicide. I told you that."

"I know what you told me, but new evidence has been

introduced. Her death had been reopened as a murder case."

Alexis stared at him in shock—or anger. He wasn't sure which.

"You've been named as a suspect in the murder," he said.

"Me? That can't be. You'd best check your source of information, Tague."

"My source is accurate. If you're still keeping secrets, now's the time to level with me, Alexis. You owe me the truth."

Fury darkened her eyes and tightened her muscles. "I owe you nothing. You're as bad as the others, Tague Lambert. Worse. You engage my son. You talk of trust. But deep down you think I'm capable of murder."

"I didn't say that." He reached for her hands, but she shoved them into his chest.

"I don't need your kind of help, Tague. I want you out of my life."

"You're talking crazy now," he said. "Be at the truck in fifteen minutes or I pull out without you."

"Go to hell." Tears rolled down her cheeks.

He grabbed her and pulled her into his arms. He hadn't planned it, but all of a sudden their lips met. Passion ripped through him, sending blood rushing to his head until he was dizzy with desire.

She pushed away, but he could see that same need in her eyes and it frightened as much as pleased him.

"*Please* be at the truck in fifteen minutes, Alexis," he whispered, requesting this time instead of demanding. "We need to get out of here before Hampton decides to show up in person."

"I didn't kill Lena."

"I believe you."

He prayed it was his brain that had come to that conclusion and not the need for her that was quickly surging out of control.

"LUNCH IN AUSTIN works great," Jackson Phelps said. "I'll meet you at the restaurant at 1:30. You can fill me in on a few details and we'll decide if this works for both of us. In the meantime, I think Alexis should turn off her phone or at least take no calls from Hampton or anyone else with the Dallas Police Department. I'd avoid calls from Sheriff Garcia, as well."

"I'll give her that word," Tague said.

By the time Jackson hung up the phone a few minutes later, his mind was reeling. Murder, kidnapping, mayhem and a Hollywood starlet with at least two aliases. If that wasn't exciting, he'd be working with Tague Lambert and an unlimited expense account. This should be a hell of a case.

The call had been brief, but extremely informative. After playing phone tag, Tague had called while pumping gas at a service station about halfway between Dallas and Austin.

Alexis Beranger—aka Melinda Ryan—and her kidnapped stepson had been in the restroom leaving Tague free to summarize the situation unfiltered.

Jackson's unofficial assessment was that the B-list actress was neck deep in crap and was counting on Tague Lambert using a gold-coated shovel to dig her out.

He'd know more when he talked to both of them at the Tex-Mex grill Jackson had suggested for lunch. The food was good and it was near his office in case they needed privacy. He wasn't sure how much Tague wanted to say in front of the kid and Alexis.

Jackson typed in "Melinda Ryan" and pulled up pages of pertinent links. He checked out a few pictures first. Easy to see how she'd gotten Tague's and Scott Hayden's attention. She was hot enough to go on the danger list for melting the polar ice caps.

He quickly moved to links related to the kidnapping. The internet was always a good place to start, but most information gleaned from the web wasn't sacrosanct.

Fortunately, Phelps had access to sites the average Joe didn't. Police networks. FBI files. And a few sites his hacking skills could get him on.

But his real work was done in the field. He had friends in low and high places and an uncanny ability to tell when a person was lying to him, especially if he was looking them in the eye. He couldn't wait to meet Alexis and talk to her in person.

He spent the next half hour on the phone collecting the inside scoop on the death of Lena Fox Hayden. Apparently, Lena's sister had persuaded the D.A. to take a second look at the autopsy.

They'd discovered enough to change the cause of death from suicide to murder.

It was easy to see why Alexis had surfaced as the number one suspect. Lena Fox's body was barely cold when Alexis had become the very wealthy director's fourth wife.

But was Scott's billions the draw for Alexis or had it always been the kid? Or perhaps Alexis had thought the legendary director could make her a star?

Whatever her motives, the honeymoon had ended early and badly.

Jackson searched another fifteen minutes before he stumbled onto a few bytes of information that stopped him in his tracks. He read it twice to make sure he'd read it correctly and then worked frantically to validate the claims.

If this turned out to be true, it proved that everything Alexis had told Tague was based on a colossal lie.

This just kept getting better and better.

TAGUE PUSHED THE last bite of his loaded beef fajita into his mouth. His attention had already wandered from the conversation Jackson Phelps and Alexis were having about raising kids.

Tommy had instigated the topic with his first meltdown of the day, bawling like he was in dire pain when Alexis wouldn't let him play with the colorful saltshaker.

Alexis took Tommy's little tantrums all in stride, or at least she seemed to. Tague was still trying to figure her out.

He'd known her for less than twenty-four hours, yet he'd spent more consecutive time with her than any other woman in his life, except for his family. With her he'd known more angst, more frustration, more irritation and far more trepidation than any other.

Even more disturbing were the sensual urges she stirred in him. The attraction persisted and grew stronger as the tension between them intensified.

And the kiss that should never have happened had knocked him totally off-kilter. Durk may have called it right. There was no way to maintain strict objectivity when dealing with a gorgeous, sexy woman like Alexis.

The sanest option for both him and Alexis might be for him to step aside and put her solely in the hands of

Meghan Sinclair. She was smart. She had a reputation for knowing her stuff. She was a professional. And she was a woman.

Temptation wouldn't blur her view of a situation that became more convoluted with each new development.

"I'm not sure how much longer I can keep Tommy occupied in the high chair," Alexis said. "If you guys want to talk in private, maybe you should grab another table now that some of the lunch crowd has left."

"I have another suggestion," Jackson said. "My office is only a ten-minute drive from here. I have a TV, a sofa and a desk in the reception office. Nothing fancy, but Tommy and you can wait there in relative comfort while Tague and I go over a few details of the case."

"Good idea," Tague said. "We'll follow you."

"I have an even better idea," Alexis said. "Why don't I ride with Jackson? That way he and I can have a few minutes to discuss my case without Tommy around."

Suspicion struck with the speed of light. If Tague discovered this was some kind of shifty maneuver to persuade Jackson to keep something from Tague, it would be the last straw. He'd fund the investigation for a week, as promised, but he'd cut any personal attachments right now.

He motioned to the waiter for the bill and paid the tab while Alexis wiped jelly from Tommy's sticky hands. She'd brought his sandwich with her. Whatever else she might be, she was a good mother to Tommy, the only mother he knew. If worst came to worst, the trauma of losing her would be a big blow to the kid's development process.

Jackson led the way out of the restaurant and into the parking lot. Alexis walked beside Tague.

"You don't mind my riding with Jackson, do you? I mean it's not like I'm going to convince him to drive me across the border during a ten-minute ride."

"Don't you think Tommy is going to scream when you ride off and leave him with me?"

"I doubt it. You're the yee-haw horsey man. But if you're uncomfortable with this, just say so. It's not that big of a deal."

He was uncomfortable with it, but it was hard to preach trust to her when he demonstrated none.

But he was through playing games. If he found out she was lying to him about Lena or anything else, he would call this whole thing off. He might be a sucker for an actress in distress but he refused to play the role of fool.

JACKSON STARTED THE engine in his gray Mercedes and backed out of his parking space. He trusted the beautiful woman sitting next to him about as much as he trusted a politician at reelection time. That didn't mean he wasn't interested in what she had to say or why she was so eager to talk to him alone.

He decided to wait and let her start the conversation. The wait was less than thirty seconds.

She buckled her seat belt and then shifted in her seat so that she faced him. "How long have you known Tague?"

"Almost as long as you have. Today's lunch was our first meeting. You must have done quite a number on him to elicit this level of monetary and personal involvement in just twenty-four hours."

"Is that what he told you, that I'd 'done a number on him'?" Indignation sharpened her tone.

"No. That was strictly an assumption on my part."

"It's obvious you don't care for me, Jackson. That's fine. I don't care that much for your attitude, either. But I'm not the one hiring you."

"I don't let my personal feelings for a subject affect my job performance. So what's on your mind?"

"What kind of trouble can Tague get into for helping me?"

That wasn't the question he was expecting. "Harboring a known fugitive from the law is a felony. He could face jail time."

"Why would anyone risk that for a person he barely knows?"

"Tague believes in you, or at least he desperately wants to. Apparently, he's the kind of guy who believes in doing the right thing, no matter the cost. Not many men like that around these days."

"You obviously think he's making a mistake by helping me."

"I don't question my client's motives. I'm a detective, not a judge. But I never coddle a client. I will give Tague the straight scoop on everything I discover, whether it's what he wants to hear or not."

"Then do Tague and me both a favor. Convince Tague to drop the investigation and to pretend he never met me. I'll take Tommy and get out of his life. He'll never see or hear from me again. No one will ever know that he was aware of my true identity."

"I'm afraid I can't do that, Alexis."

"Why not?"

"Because at his point I think you're guilty as hell and if I persuade him to let you walk away, that would mean I'm aiding and abetting a fugitive."

"You're wrong about my being guilty of anything except bad judgment, Jackson Phelps. Dead wrong. But don't let that stop you from condemning me. It's never stopped anyone else."

"If I'm wrong, and you're innocent, then I'll prove that, too. But we're jumping the gun here. Tague hasn't officially hired me yet."

"If he asks, what will you tell him about me?"

"That either you're lying to him or he's lying to me."

"Tague won't lie to you."

"I agree."

"What is it you think I've lied about?"

"Your relationship to Tommy."

He pulled into his reserved parking spot in front of his office. Tague parked right behind him. Conversation with Alexis ceased.

But if her stare could kill, Jackson would be drawing his last breath about now.

To Tague's surprise, not only did Tommy not scream as they left without his mother, but he was asleep before they'd gone two blocks.

Fifteen minutes later, Tommy was continuing his nap on a worn green sofa in Jackson's reception room with Alexis watching over him. Tague was sitting in an uncomfortable chair facing Jackson, who was propped against the back side of a large and extremely cluttered desk.

"Alexis looks upset," Tague said. "Did you two get into an argument on the way over?"

"We talked, but there was no argument. Just a meet-

ing of the minds. I have dug up some significant information to add to what you already know, though."

"Let's hear it."

"Maybe you should sit down first."

Chapter Ten

"Lena Fox is not Tommy's birth mother."

"Here we go again." Tague leaned back in his chair and prepared for the worst. "Did Alexis tell you that?"

"No, and I haven't had the chance to fully verify the veracity of the statement, but I'm almost certain it's factual."

"How certain is almost certain?"

"According to her medical records, Lena had a dirty abortion when she was sixteen. Complications developed and she ended up requiring surgery that left her unable to bear children."

"But that was years ago. What with all the changes modern science has made in the field, isn't it possible that the prognosis changed?"

"Lena's womb was removed."

"So if Lena didn't give birth to Tommy, who did?"

"I don't have that information as yet, but I suggest you talk to Alexis about that."

"I guess she would be the obvious one to go to for answers about Scott Hayden's son, isn't she?" It was a rhetorical question and he didn't expect an answer. Nor did he try to hide his irritation and cynicism.

But he had to take some of the blame. He'd stared into

Alexis's beautiful, lying eyes and licked up the deceit the same way Tommy had gone after that lollipop yesterday.

"I'll sit with the kid if you and Alexis want to talk in my office," Jackson offered.

"No. The conversation can wait until we get to the hunting camp."

"Are you still interested in pursuing the investigation?" Jackson asked.

"I'll fund it, but as soon as I can make arrangements for paid security to stay with Alexis, I'm going back to the ranch."

"Do you think she's in danger?"

"Frankly, I don't know what to think anymore. She claims she received a call from Scott Hayden the night of the carjacking."

"Whoa. I must be missing something here. She's wanted by the police for suspicion of murdering Scott's third wife and for kidnapping his child. Yet they keep in touch and he doesn't bother to tell the police how to find her?"

"Sounds bizarre, I know. It did to me, too. But give Alexis a few minutes and she can come up with an explanation for anything."

"If she can explain that and make it sound rational, she should be a shoo-in for an Oscar."

"I have to admit she looked terrified after the call and was ready to bolt," Tague said. "That's what prompted her to finally agree to my offer to spend the night at the ranch."

Jackson steepled his fingers. "So spending the night at the ranch was your idea?"

"Right. Alexis did her best to get rid of me. She still is, for that matter."

"I noticed. She wanted me to convince you to let her take the kid and head for Mexico."

"So that's why she wanted to ride over with you?"

"And she wanted to know how much trouble you can get in for protecting her."

"The truth is, I'm not surprised at either of those things."

"But back to the phone call from Scott," Jackson said. "What was that about?"

"Reportedly all he said was that she knew what he wanted. She figured he'd located her and would burst through the door at any second."

"And that was it?" Jackson asked. "Just a phone call out of the blue from the man she allegedly tried to kill?"

"Like I said, it was bizarre, especially following on the heels of the carjacking."

"If he didn't give his name, I'd be more inclined to think Alexis was mistaken and that it was the carjacker who called."

"She seemed sure it was Scott, said she'd know his voice anywhere."

"Panic can play strange tricks with the mind. But if it was Scott who called, you'd best be prepared for trouble, Tague. My motto is that when you can't figure out someone's motives, it's time to worry."

Tague agreed. "That's why I'm anxious to get the investigation going at full speed. As I told you, I already have Meghan Sinclair on board. Do you have any objections to working with another private investigator?"

"Not if it's Meghan. She and I have never worked together but we've met. She's top-notch. We may prefer different methods for getting to the bottom of things, but I think we'd be compatible."

"I know you haven't had much time since my earlier phone call, but have you given any thought as to where you'd start?"

Jackson reached across his desk and picked up a sheet of paper where he'd jotted down notes. "Here's where I am. I figure that either Scott Hayden is the monster that Alexis depicted him as, or she's the mentally unbalanced woman who attacked him without provocation, set his house on fire, kidnapped his son and possibly even killed his wife."

"The son who might be more than her stepson," Tague said.

Jackson nodded in agreement. "That would open another giant can of killer worms and make Scott even more of a monster for framing her. It's been my experience that monsters don't just spring to life. They develop over time. Dig deep enough into Scott's past and we'll find out if the man is capable of heinous acts."

"Makes sense to me," Tague said. "But what if Alexis is the one who's lying?"

"We'll figure that out as we go. If she's guilty, you call the cops or talk her into turning herself in. Frankly, I have trouble believing she's squeaky-clean with all the accusations against her. But I'm willing to keep an open mind until the facts close it for me."

"Then we agree on that much. Are you ready to talk price and expectations?"

Jackson handed Tague a printed form that quoted his hourly rate and which expenses were to be paid by Tague.

"I'll give you that and a three thousand dollar bonus if you can deliver the results by next Monday," Tague said. "Time is of the essence. I'm holding a kidnapper hostage."

"Either that, or she's holding you hostage," Jackson said. "How about I start on my homework tonight and meet you at the camp in the morning? I'd like to hear Alexis's justification for the kidnapping from her. We can also discuss strategy a bit more. If Meghan can make it, all the better. How about 9:00 a.m.?"

"How about 6:00 a.m.?" Tague said. "I work on rancher's hours."

"Six it is."

In the meantime, Tague planned to have a long discussion with Alexis about how a woman without a womb gave birth to Tommy.

THE HUNTING CAMP was far more lavish than Alexis had imagined. The decor and design had a rustic flair, but all the modern conveniences were present, including big-screen TVs, a commercial oven, grill and cooktop, a huge den with leather chairs and sofas, and a giant stone fireplace that they wouldn't be needing in July.

The only drawback was that she was surrounded by wild animals that didn't move but simply stared at her with glassy eyes. Moose, elk, bear and caribou scrutinized her every move as if preparing to pounce from their respective lookouts.

Even here in the kitchen, a huge blue-and-silver fish looked as if it might flop from the wall and into the frying pan at any second.

In spite of the stuffed and mounted menagerie, the lodge had a lot going for it. It was tucked away in a setting so serene and isolated that had she not been so on edge, she would have felt safer than she had in months.

Now all she felt was the anxiety of waiting for Tague to ask about Lena. She knew the question and the resulting argument about trust and honesty were coming. She just didn't know when and the suspense was churning in her stomach.

It was one more lie she'd have to explain. One more personal failing that Tague wouldn't understand. How could he comprehend her insecurities when he'd lived a charmed life since the day he was born? Always cosseted. Always knowing where he fit in the grand scheme of life.

She rinsed Tommy's empty bottle, thankful he'd settled down and gone to sleep so quickly in yet another strange bedroom. Fortunately, he was captivated by the mounted animals, especially after Tague lifted him up to touch each one and see that they were harmless.

Tommy had never taken to any man as quickly as he'd taken to Tague. Nor had she. That made disappointing him again especially painful. But now she just wanted to get it over with.

She walked to the back door, opened it and stepped outside. There was a slight breeze, but the heavily shaded Texas Hill Country setting was a welcome relief from the stifling heat they'd left in Dallas.

Tague must have agreed. He was relaxing in one of the teak Adirondack chairs grouped around a built-in fire pit just a few yards from the house. She turned to go back inside, but changed her mind. The tension was driving her mad.

She marched over and perched on the edge of one of the chairs. She'd rehearsed what she'd say ever since they'd left Jackson Phelps's office. She tried to think of how she'd planned to start. When she couldn't, she simply blurted out the truth.

"I gave birth to Tommy."

Tague met her gaze and held it. "Is that a fact or is that merely what it says in your script? Time to throw another crumb of information to the naive cowboy?"

She deserved his attitude, but it still riled her. She stared down his glare. "Do you want to hear this or not?"

He finished the beer he was holding and dropped the empty bottle to the grass. "Is it the truth?"

"Yes, but it's not what you think."

"It never is when I'm dealing with you."

"You're not making this easy."

"I'm not the one who dishes out information in piecemeal fashion, manufacturing it as I go."

"I was wrong not to explain everything, but it's not like we're old friends, Tague. I barely know you. And I didn't ask for your help."

"Point made. Would you like a beer?"

"No, thank you."

"I would."

He returned a minute later with a longneck brew. He took a gulp before looking her way again. "So you gave birth to Scott Hayden's son before Lena killed herself or was murdered. Your being the mother of Lena's husband's son must have caused a few fireworks around the breakfast table."

"I didn't say I was Tommy's mother. I said I gave birth to him."

"I'm apparently missing something in the translation."

"Lena couldn't have children because of a medical

condition. She begged me to supply my womb for her and Scott's embryo."

"And you agreed to that?"

"Not at first. I was still clinging to visions of becoming a great actress. I didn't want stretch marks or morning sickness or labor pains."

"What changed your mind?" Tague asked.

"Lena. She was so desperate to have a child. I couldn't say no to her dreams for my selfish reasons. Besides, at the time I was stupid enough to believe she and Scott were in love and that they'd be wonderful parents."

"Weren't they in love?"

"To the contrary. They were having significant marital problems. Lena thought that by giving Scott the one thing no other woman had, she could hold on to him."

"Did he want a child?"

"Absolutely. His vanity and egotism demanded he pass on his self-perceived genius to a descendant."

"Sounds like a real charmer," Tague said.

"You'd see right through him," she admitted. "Lena didn't. Neither did I until the truth was too brutal and blatant to ignore."

Tague took another sip of his beer. "Did Lena ever complain of monstrous behavior on his part?"

"Not to me."

"Then what do you think their problems were?"

"Sex and drugs."

"A shortage of one and an abundance of the other?" Tague asked.

"No. There was an abundance of both. Scott was mostly a recreational user. Lena was on the fast track to becoming a full-fledged addict. And Scott had told her he was in love with someone else."

"You?" Tague asked.

"Yes, but neither Lena nor I guessed that—or if Lena did, she never admitted it to me. By the time I realized their marriage was on the fast track to divorce, their child had been growing inside me for six months."

Oddly, admitting the truth after so long was somewhat cathartic. Slipping back into the past wasn't. She struggled to keep the worst of the memories from pulling her back into the nightmare.

"Were you and Lena friends before you agreed to be the surrogate womb?"

"I thought we were. It turns out I was the intended 'womb' from the very beginning. I even agreed to her specifications that I hide my pregnancy while she hid her lack of a pregnant body."

"How did you get mixed up with these sick people in the first place?"

"It started out innocently enough. I went to a casting call for a historical romantic thriller Scott Hayden was going to produce and direct. I was so nervous about reading for him that I messed up the lines. I was shocked when I got a callback a week later."

"Did you get the part?"

"No, but he had me act out an entire scene in costume. Not the official costume, but one he'd provided so that he could get a real sense of the performance. At least that's what he'd claimed."

"And this time you were terrific."

"No. Bottom line, the Great One said I didn't project the kind of terror he was looking for."

"How did you go from losing a role to becoming Lena's pretend friend and the incubator for their fetus?"

"I got an invitation to their Malibu beach house

the following weekend. Invitations to a Scott Jeffery Hayden weekend are about as rare for wannabes like me as receiving the golden grail by FedEx. Of course, I accepted."

"Of course."

"Lena spent hours with me. At the end of the weekend, she said that Scott was convinced I had talent but that it needed nurturing. She was willing to devote a few months of her life to provide that. All she wanted in return was for me to live in her guesthouse and keep her company while Scott was on location in Paris."

Tague finished his beer, dropped the empty bottle to the grass next to the other one and massaged the back of his neck. "Apparently, you took her up on the offer."

"I moved in the very next week, sure that was exactly what I needed to soar me to stardom. And then I let her talk me into carrying their child. I'm not that naive anymore."

"Is naiveté your excuse for marrying Scott Hayden just two months after Lena died?"

"No. That was love."

"Were you having an affair with him while Lena was still alive?"

"I never had an affair with him. And the love wasn't for him. It was for Tommy. From the moment I first felt him move inside me, all my priorities changed."

"How so?"

"He became my life. When I gave birth to him, the bond grew even stronger. I heard his first cries, rocked him to sleep, stayed up with him when he was sick."

"Where was Lena?"

"Mostly she kept to her room. By then her marriage was in shambles and she'd turned totally to drugs. Scott asked me to stay on in the guesthouse and take care of Tommy and I jumped at the opportunity."

"But you weren't romantically involved with him?"

"No, but I knew he was interested in me in a sexual way. I convinced myself I could handle his advances. All that really mattered to me was not losing contact with Tommy. He was my son in every way that mattered except DNA."

"So when Lena died, you married Scott and became Mrs. Scott Jeffery number four?"

"Scott wanted a wife and a mother for Tommy. If not me, it would be someone else, and in that case he made it clear I'd never see Tommy again."

Tears filled Alexis's eyes. She turned away so Tague wouldn't see them. She'd made so many mistakes. Tommy was the only good thing to come from them.

"I thought I could learn to love Scott—for Tommy's sake. I couldn't. I thought I was hiding my true feelings until one night I cried when we had sex. After that, he never touched me again except in anger. That's when I realized I'd married a monster."

Tears began to stream down her cheeks. She dabbed at her eyes with the backs of her fists but it did little to slow the flow.

Tague stepped behind her and wrapped his arms around her waist. "I'm sorry for the way I reacted. You've been through enough without having me turn sarcastic."

"It's not you. It's everything. All the mistakes. All the ways I've messed up my life and Tommy's." Shudders shook her body and she couldn't stop sobbing.

Tague tugged her around to face him and held her in his arms. "I've never been good at dealing with a crying woman, but I don't think you should fight the tears, Alexis. It seems you've locked enough inside you to last a lifetime."

When she finally stopped crying, she pulled away. "It's just that I love Tommy so much."

"I promised to do what I can to help you, Alexis. I still will, but even if we find evidence to back up your claim that your husband tried to kill you, that won't automatically lead to your getting custody of Tommy."

"I know that. But there is a way you could make sure Tommy stays with me. All you have to do is help me get to Mexico before Hampton alerts every law enforcement agency in the state that I'm in the area."

"You might escape the law, but Scott would eventually find you. You must know that. And when he does, you'd have to face him on your own. I can't let you do that."

He dropped his arms from around her. "I can't change the past. Neither can you. But that doesn't mean you have to blow the future. Now let's go inside and see what we can rustle up for dinner. It's been a long, long time since lunch and I'm starved."

"You know, Tague, you're a lot better at handling a crying woman than you give yourself credit for."

"It's not me. It's the beer talking." Tague gathered up his empties. "Just for the record, would you go back to acting if you got the chance?"

"Not in a million years. I'd look for something to do that I'm good at."

"Like milking beef cattle," he teased.

"Maybe."

In a New York second, if the cows came with a man like Tague.

Tague forked the bacon and admired Alexis's slender hands as she slid the razor-sharp knife through the bright red beefsteak tomato they'd picked up at the market.

"Careful with the knife," he warned. "Hunters tend to keep all their blades honed to perfection, even those in the storage block."

"Please tell me that no one used this to butcher one of those animals mounted on the wall."

"Most of those were killed in the Northwest. The two bucks in the den area were killed here on the property, but I can assure you that no one used a kitchen knife on them, at least not before the meat was ready to cook."

She spread a generous dab of mayonnaise on two slices of bread. "Do you hunt?"

"I have, but fishing's my sport of choice. My dad did a lot of hunting in his younger years, but I think he and his buddies mostly used this place for male bonding. This is the first time anyone's been up here since his death."

"This wasn't what I pictured when you said 'camp.'"

"What were you expecting?"

"Gas lanterns, bedrolls, cooking over an open fire. Not that I'm complaining, but this is sheer luxury. Nothing's missing but a crew of servants."

"I gave them the week off."

"You're kidding?"

"Well, there's not actually a crew, but there is a man and his wife who've been taking care of the place for years. Otherwise, it would be overrun with spiders, scorpions, lizards and maybe a rattlesnake or two. This is still Texas, you know."

"And if I encounter any of those creatures, they'll hear me scream all the way to Austin." She reached for the lettuce she'd just washed and pulled off a couple of crisp leaves.

"You know, Tague, I know you're wealthy. I've seen your ranch and the luxury you have here. But I still have trouble thinking of you as one of the Lamberts I read about in the society pages."

"Then don't. I never do."

"You're so normal."

"Isn't that a synonym for 'boring'?"

"'Normal' was probably not the best word choice. You're easy to be with—and you listen. Really listen."

"I'll take that as a compliment. Now let's eat. I'm starving."

They carried their food to the oversize den and settled on a sofa that faced a wall of windows. The sun had slipped below the horizon and twilight was creeping from the shadows like a caressing blanket.

The beauty and the peaceful setting were wasted on Tague. He'd arrived at the camp ready to turn her safety and the investigation over to others and drive back to the ranch. But as soon as she'd started explaining the situation with Lena, he'd fallen completely under her spell. She was like a liqueur with the power to intoxicate in a single drop.

He was half-finished with his sandwich when his phone rang. The caller ID read "Carolina Lambert." He had a disturbing premonition that she was not calling just to say good-night.

The second he heard her voice, he knew that his instincts for trouble were still healthy and intact.

Chapter Eleven

"I'm worried about Alexis, Tague."

So was Tague. If Alexis wasn't taking him for a ride down deception road, she was in trouble so deep a bull-dozer couldn't dig her out. But his mother knew nothing of that and he hoped to keep it that way for a few days longer.

"Mother, don't you have enough things to worry about without looking for more?"

"I'm serious, Tague. I just got off the phone from talking with Detective Gerald Hampton with the Dal-las police force. He's the detective who's investigating the carjacking."

That bit of news rattled his nerves. "What did Hamp-ton want?"

"He said he's been trying to reach Alexis on her cell phone all day. She isn't answering and she hasn't been to her apartment. He was hoping we knew how to get in touch with her. He says it's extremely important that he reach her at once."

"What did you tell him?"

"That she left here this morning, planning to rent a car and drive to a friend's house in Tulsa for a few days. He seemed surprised about that."

Tague breathed easier. If the detective had mentioned that Alexis was wanted for kidnapping and possibly murder, his mother wouldn't be worried about unanswered phones. Which meant Hampton either didn't know Alexis's identity yet or had chosen not to share that info with his mother.

"I'm sure Alexis is fine," he said. "She's probably having such a great time with her friend, she didn't bother turning on her cell phone."

"Do you have her phone number?"

"No," he lied. "But I'm sure she'll call the detective as soon as she gets his messages."

"I think you should call the detective, Tague. Find out why he seems so desperate to reach her."

"I suspect you're reading way too much into this. Hampton probably just wants her to pick the carjacker out of a lineup."

"I think it's more than that, Tague. I think she's in some kind of trouble. I could hear it in the detective's voice. If she is, we have to find a way to help her and her adorable son."

"Did you ask the detective why he was trying to get in touch with her?"

"Yes, but he said he wasn't at liberty to say. That in itself means it can't be good."

"Not necessarily. I think we should stay out of this. It's Alexis's business, not ours. The carjacker has been arrested and she's safe. That's good enough for me."

"You don't know that she's safe. I think I'll call Winston Harris. Hugh and he were great friends. They hunted and fished together."

"I'm sure it's not necessary to bring the chief of police into this, Mother."

But he knew she would if he didn't promise to do something. "I'll give the detective a call," he assured her, "even though I don't think it's necessary."

"I want to know what you find out, Tague."

"I'll call you back once I've talked to him, but it may be tomorrow before I can get him. If you don't hear from me within the hour, go to bed and get some sleep."

"I'll try, but I'm telling you there's something wrong. I have a sixth sense about these things."

Unfortunately, she frequently did.

Tague broke the connection and went in search of Alexis. He found her rinsing the dishes and loading them into the dishwasher.

"I wasn't eavesdropping, but I couldn't help hearing enough to know you were talking to Carolina," she said. "Is something wrong?"

"She's concerned about you. Did you get calls from Detective Hampton today?"

"Several, but that was after Jackson Phelps suggested I not answer calls from him. He didn't leave a message. Why?"

"Apparently he called the ranch to see if you were still there. Mother told him you'd gone to visit a friend in Tulsa."

The forks she was rinsing slipped from her fingers and clattered into the sink. "He must have identified my fingerprints from the car."

"Don't jump to conclusions. I'll give him a call and see if I can find out what's going on."

"Should you talk to Jackson first?"

"Jackson's a private investigator. I'm interested in what he uncovers, but I'm calling the shots."

"Then go for it, cowboy."

Tague made the call. The detective answered immediately. Tague identified himself and got down to business. "My mother said you're looking for Alexis Lambert. Is anything wrong?"

"You could say that. All hell's broken loose here. I didn't want to get into the gore with your mother, but it's a damn good thing Alexis went home with you last night."

Tague's muscles tightened. "What happened?"

"I went by her apartment this afternoon when I couldn't get her on the phone. When I got there, I detected an all too familiar and extremely unpleasant odor. I had the property manager give me a key."

Tague had a good idea where this was going. "What did you find?"

"One of the bloodiest crime scenes I've run into in years. Blood was splattered from the floor to the ceiling. Two skulls were crushed like overripe pineapples."

Two skulls that might have been Alexis's and Tommy's had he left them there alone last night. His insides rolled as listened to the rest of what Hampton had to say.

By the time the conversation was finished, his stomach was calmer, but his determination had solidified to the consistency of solid granite.

He reached for Alexis's hand.

Trepidation was etched into every line of her face. "This is about Scott, isn't it? What's he done?"

The questions flew from her mouth before he had time to even begin to answer. "Let's go outside to talk," he said. "I need some air." And time to assimilate the tale of horror he'd just heard.

"Let me check on Tommy first and I'll be right with you."

"Better bring that beer for yourself that you turned down earlier. You'll need it."

"Two young men were beaten to death with a baseball bat in my apartment." Alexis repeated what Tague had just told her as she struggled to wrap her head around the brutal crime. "Why were they there?"

Tague paced, wearing a beaten path in the grass with his heavy boots. "That hasn't been established. Nor have the victims' identities. The DPD's Crime Scene Unit was in your apartment for most of the afternoon, but according to Hampton, even they're having trouble making sense of the bloody chaos."

"Obviously, they don't have the fingerprint report back from my car. If they did he'd have surely mentioned that, as well."

"The car's likely been moved to the back burner after this. Besides, they feel confident they have the right perpetrator in jail for that."

"If I'd stayed in the apartment last night…" Her words trailed into silence as her thoughts took form.

Tague reached for her hand again, this time tugging her to her feet. "I would have camped outside your door before I left you alone, not that I would have been expecting this. Let's walk while I tell you the rest. I think better on my feet."

"There's more?"

"A little."

"I don't want to leave sight of the house with Tommy inside. In fact, it's all I can do not to wake him up just so that I can feel his sweet arms around my neck."

"I know. But he's safe and you're safe and I promise I'll do everything in my power to make sure it stays that way."

They walked slowly, past the fire pit and a couple of young cedars, finally stopping at a picnic table at the edge of the clearing. She looked back at the lodge, amazed at how safe and welcoming its rustic cypress siding looked in the moonlight.

But no place was safe for her as long as Scott Jeffery Hayden was alive. Even the baseball bat as a weapon sounded like him. There were guns in the Malibu house, but he always slept with a bat beneath the edge of his bed.

"You said there was more," she said. "What have you left out?"

"There were four sets of footprints in the blood."

"Two against two," Alexis said. "Evenly numbered, but no fair fight."

"Hampton apparently has no clue at this point whether the four men came together and then got into the deadly head bashing or if two men were waiting there to ambush the other two."

"But why in my apartment?"

"No one seems to know and that's what worries me most about the slaughter," Tague said. "I'm hoping one of my investigators can get his hands on the official CSU report. That may tell us something."

"Scott has to figure in this somehow," Alexis said. "He calls me and the violence breaks loose."

"But it was his call that may have saved you," Tague said. "You flew into a flurry of packing after that. I've never seen anyone clear closets and drawers that quickly."

"Because I expected him to show up any second. Now

that I think about it, I bet he was just outside someone's door that he thought was mine. By the time he realized he was at the wrong apartment, I was gone."

"Those are all assumptions."

"They make sense. Scott waited on me and then when I didn't show up, he got high on cocaine and flew into one of his rages."

"This wasn't just a barroom-type brawl, Alexis. It was a massacre. This is far more likely connected to the carjacker and his Death Knight pals than it is to Scott."

Nothing Tague could say would convince her that Scott didn't have a hand in this. And he wouldn't give up—not until she was in jail and he had Tommy back with him. Nothing Tague could do would change that.

Tague was brave, valiant and honest. But Scott was ruthless. And it was only in the movies that the good guy always won.

"It's still not too late to walk away from me, Tague. Pretend you never met me. Go back to your life."

He pulled her into his arms and held her close. She felt his heart beating against hers, felt the strength in his muscles and the protectiveness in his touch.

"I'm not going anywhere, Alexis. Not until this is settled. Not until you're safe. Now let's go inside and get ready for bed. Six o'clock comes early."

But between now and then she'd have nightmares to survive, nightmares that were on the verge of becoming reality once again.

"Stay with me tonight, Tague. Just until I fall asleep. I know it sounds childish but I don't want to be alone."

"I'll be there as long as you need me."

But even that would change. It always did.

TAGUE KICKED THE clods of red clay earth from his boots and stepped back inside the house. It wouldn't be daylight for another hour, but he'd woken early and been too restless to stay inside.

He wasn't convinced that Scott Hayden had anything to do with the murders in Alexis's apartment. The guy was a respected director. He didn't go around bashing men's heads in with a bat. Even in Hollywood, that wouldn't fly.

But he had dangled his own son from a balcony and tried to burn Alexis to death. That made Tague uneasy enough that he'd made a call to the same protective service they'd used when Damien's wife, Emma, had been in danger.

Cork was meeting with them at the ranch this morning. They'd make certain that Scott Hayden did not show his face at the Bent Pine Ranch.

The more difficult call would be explaining this to his mother. But Carolina was a sharp woman. She'd already figured out that Alexis was in danger. She'd deal with having extra protection around the house and at the ranch.

That was a start, but not enough. Hiring private investigators was all well and good, but Tague was starting to feel like a coach and he was hungry to take the field. He needed to be in on the action. The problem would be finding someone he trusted to stay with Alexis.

Normally, he'd hire a protection service, just like he had for the Bent Pine Ranch, but that service and the others he was familiar with were owned by retired Texas Rangers or police officers. Chances were too great that one of them would recognize Alexis as Melinda Ryan.

He slapped his Stetson against his thighs a couple of

times and then set it on the shelf. His dad used to keep at least a half dozen hunting caps on that shelf, ones he'd collected from all around the world. The caps were packed away now, along with the memories of weekends spent out here with just his father and his two brothers.

His dad had called this the man's world, a place where they didn't have to follow women's rules like keeping your feet off the furniture and always remembering to put the toilet seat down.

This was where his dad had given him the sex talk and the drug talk and the know-when-to-hold-'em-and-when-to-fold-'em lecture.

He couldn't help but wonder what bigger-than-life Hugh Lambert would have said about Alexis Beranger. It would likely be the same things Tague had already told himself.

Stay objective. Don't take unnecessary risks. Don't fall for a married woman who's wanted by the law and who never seems to give you the straight scoop on anything—at least not until she's caught in a lie.

He probably wouldn't have followed his father's advice any better than he'd followed his own. He stayed objective until she opened her mouth. Then he bought every word that came from those full, luscious lips.

He was trying not to take risks, but how could he avoid risks when he had no idea what he was really up against? The two murders had no obvious connection with Scott Hayden or the carjacker, but it was inconceivable that they were random in light of all that was going on.

And telling him not to fall for Alexis was like telling a teenage boy to stop thinking about girls. The attraction was devastating. The need to protect her was overwhelming.

He hadn't dared lay beside her while she fell asleep last night. The need to hold her and kiss her and make love to her had consumed him when he was merely sitting in a chair near her bed.

And this was only day three of their relationship. How much more temptation could he handle without blowing a fuse?

He started a pot of coffee and then pulled a package of biscuits from the freezer. His two investigators were due to arrive in thirty minutes. He might as well fix enough breakfast for them, too.

He laid some sausage patties on the indoor grill and slid the biscuits into the oven while he waited for the coffee to finish dripping. He'd just poured a cup when his phone jangled. Probably his mother demanding to know why Cork had strangers on the ranch or one of the P.I.s letting him know they were running late.

He grabbed it without checking the caller ID. "Hello."

"Bonjour, bro."

"Damien. Good to hear from you. How's Paris?"

"French. Very French."

"How's the honeymoon going?"

"Ooh la la."

"I take it that means good?"

"I'm with Emma. How could it be anything but?"

"So how come you have time to call me?"

"I talked to Durk and Mother."

"That explains it."

"Who is this Alexis Beranger and what's her story?"

"How much have you already heard?"

"That she's married and wanted by the law from

Durk. That she's a wonderful lady who needs help from Mother. I'm guessing the truth falls somewhere in between."

"Both of those are probably accurate assessments." Tague gave him the details in rapid-fire style since he was expecting Meghan and Jackson any minute now. He culminated with the two murders.

"It sounds like you have your hands full," Damien said.

"I'm handling it."

"Yes, but I'm missing all the action. Besides I owe you one since you were right there for me when Emma was in danger. Emma's on the hotel phone right now checking flights. With luck we can be back in Texas by tonight—your time."

"I appreciate the offer of help, but I don't want you to cut your honeymoon short."

"You'd do it for me. Besides I've had enough croissants. I'm ready for steak and eggs, and biscuits smothered in gravy."

"I guess Durk told you I'm at the hunting camp."

"He did. We're flying into Austin. We'll rent a car there and drive to the camp. So don't mention to Mother that we're leaving Paris. By the way, I'm assuming you're making sure Mom, Aunt Sybil and Grandma aren't in any danger."

"I've got that covered, but I don't think you want to bring Emma into the middle of Alexis's problems."

"You're right. I don't. But Emma's not good about taking no for an answer. She says if anyone can understand what Alexis is going through, it's her."

"She has a point. So I guess I'll see you two tonight."

"Hopefully before too late."

And with Damien at the camp, Tague would be free to fly to California and see what he could uncover about the monster director who was married to the woman Tague might never get off his mind.

SCOTT SNEAKED IN the back door of his Malibu estate in the predawn hours, hoping none of the servants were awake to witness his arrival. Not that they'd suspect he'd just flown in from Dallas in his private jet.

Nothing had gone as planned. The two thugs had come at him and Bronco so unexpectedly he'd barely had time to dodge the acid.

Bronco hadn't. A spray of the stringent liquid had landed on his forearm, eating the flesh in an instant. His terrifying scream had sent the men running from Alexis's abandoned bedroom.

But Scott had been too quick for them. Fueled by fury and fear, he'd dived for the baseball bat he'd brought in with him. He never carried a gun. His hands shook more than ever of late, and he was more likely to drop a pistol than send a bullet into someone's brain.

The long-term use of cocaine and other illegal substances had begun to take their toll on him. At least that's what the doctors blamed his increasingly dramatic mood swings on. They were getting harder and harder to control. Sometimes he didn't even remember them.

But he couldn't give up cocaine. Before he'd tried it, he'd been a nobody. He'd hated that and hated the people around him who were making their mark without possessing nearly the intellect he had. The drug had set his genius free.

But he'd learn to control it as soon as Alexis was arrested and convicted of Lena's death. No way was he going to let the cops pin that on him.

He was Scotty Jeffery Hayden, genius director. And that would all die with him.

The good thing tonight was that Bronco had fought right along with him. Bronco was a giant, all muscles, no fat. And loyal to the core.

Scott dragged himself to the bathroom. He'd slipped into the depths of fatigue where every step took effort and the sharp boundaries of his intellect blurred into foggy edges of madness.

Melinda Ryan. Sexy, young seductress who hadn't had a clue about the way she affected men. When she'd come to that first audition, she'd been too nervous to look him in the eye. But he'd watched her every move.

Her acting skills were abysmal, but he knew then he'd have to find a way to see her again. And again. And again.

Scott stepped out of his clothes and crossed the room naked. He opened the drawer next to his bed and took out the black negligee. She'd worn it for him at the second audition when he'd requested she perform in costume.

He could see her now, crossing the stage in the slinky gown, her hips swaying, her lips red and full, her eyes a mix of sapphire and midnight. She'd been the image of innocence and purity with the body of a temptress.

She hadn't been able to portray fear that day, but insecurity? Yes. She'd embraced that completely.

But not fear.

Next time she auditioned for him, she would.

And he might just invite the wealthy young cowboy she'd run off with along for the show. As soon as he found them. It was only a matter of time.

Chapter Twelve

Alexis woke to the jarring glare of beams of light sweeping across her walls. She jumped up and rushed to the window for a better look. A truck stopped in the driveway, just behind a sports car.

Jackson Phelps and Meghan Sinclair were already here and it was still dark out. What kind of nuts conducted business this time of the morning?

She glanced at the clock. Five minutes before six. Tague hadn't woken her as promised. That had probably been Tague's plan all alone. Even now, she suspected he didn't fully believe her. Who could blame him?

She padded to the bathroom, quietly closing the door behind her so that she wouldn't disturb Tommy.

She splashed some water on her face and then reluctantly stared into the mirror. The swelling had gone down around her right eye, but the flesh was still a canvas of purple and blue tints. It would have looked better concealed by makeup but there was no time. She didn't want to miss a word of what the P.I.s had to say.

She pulled on a pair of dark blue Bermuda shorts and a white cotton shirt that she tied at the waist. She finger-combed her mussed hair as she slipped into her sandals. A quick swipe of lip gloss and she decided that would have to do.

"Sorry I'm late," she said, joining the group of three in the kitchen."

"You're not late," Jackson said. "I just got here myself. Had a devil of a time finding this place. I'm surprised the wildlife can make it this far back into the sticks."

"I guess I should have given better directions," Tague said. "Did you have trouble getting here, too, Meghan?"

"No, but I've been here before. I drove out one day with Durk," she explained when they all stared at her in surprise.

"My brother mentioned the two of you were friends when he recommended you for this job," Tague said.

"It was a long time ago." Meghan turned and introduced herself to Alexis.

"Thanks for coming out this morning," Alexis said. "Though I don't usually consider it morning when the stars are still out."

"I spent the night in Austin last night and I'm an early riser," Meghan said. "Unfortunately, I usually collapse by ten. But last night I stayed up and watched part of one of your films."

"Which one?"

"Valley of the Fangs."

"You brave soul. No wonder you only made it through part of the movie. But I don't know how you found it. I thought all copies had been burned or at least banned from human consumption."

"It wasn't that bad."

"No, it was worse." They both laughed.

Alexis was pretty sure she was going to like Meghan. She wasn't wearing any makeup either, but she was stunning. Tall and willowy, with thick auburn curls cascading past her shoulders that brought out the deep green of her eyes. A spatter of freckles across the bridge of her nose only added to her natural beauty.

Tague handed Alexis a mug of steaming coffee.

"Thanks." She took a sip, craving the taste and the caffeine. "I thought you were going to wake me so that I wouldn't have to set the alarm and risk waking Tommy."

"I was about to wake you when Meghan showed up. Then I got involved in a conversation. But you didn't miss anything."

"Good."

"We can talk over breakfast," Tague said. "If anyone needs to wash up first, there are two bathrooms off the hall. The first door to the right and the fourth door to the left."

Both Meghan and Jackson took him up on the offer. Alexis sipped her coffee and tried to convince her body it was awake. "Breakfast smells wonderful. Anything I can help with?"

"It's all ready," he said. "Buffet style."

"So what's this about Meghan and your brother Durk?" Alexis asked. "Were they an item once?"

"That's the impression I get. Neither has offered details."

"She's a ten, that's for sure, and seems to have a personality to go with the looks," Alexis said.

"All I care about right now is that she has brains and is good at her job."

Minutes later they were all seated at the kitchen table with plates of food in front of them. This time the food did not claim priority, perhaps because the first topic of conversation was the bloody murders in Alexis's apartment.

"I'll get my hands on a copy of that police report," Jackson said. "When we have all the facts and the identities of the victims, we can get a better idea of what really took place."

"Have you had any luck in discovering why Lena Fox's suicide was upgraded to murder?" Tague asked.

"Not yet, but I'm working on it. I've made contact with Lena's older sister Gabrielle and I think she may agree to meet with me. I get the impression she's not too fond of Scott. I'm also checking the backgrounds of everyone who works at the Hayden house in any capacity."

"That's a quite a few people," Alexis said.

Jackson broke his biscuit in half and used it to sop up some gravy. "You could run a five-star hotel with fewer staff. You probably know some of them, Alexis."

"Scott had a high turnover rate, but I imagine a few like his bodyguard Bronco and his head housekeeper are still with him."

Meghan choked on her coffee. "His bodyguard is named Bronco?"

"That's all I ever heard him called," Alexis said. "But it could be because he's the size of a car."

"I'll try to stay on his good side," Jackson said. "Did any of the household or garden staff have issues with Lena when you lived there?"

"Most of them did at one time or another. Lena was high-maintenance. She was a perfectionist—except when she was under the influence of cocaine. In the end, that was most of the time."

"A perfectionist in what way?" Tague asked. "Her own appearance? The house? Her work?"

"All of the above, but in the end, her primary focus was on anything involving Scott. She'd insist that every detail of the preparations be precisely orchestrated on the nights Scott was expected to have dinner at home. She gave the staff directions for every aspect of the meal, right down to the fragrance of the candles and the glasses for serving her chosen aperitif."

"The staff must have loved that," Meghan said.

"Fortunately for them, Scott only ate at home a couple of nights a week."

Meghan toyed with the handle of her coffee mug. "I'm not certain I have the timelines for your life in the Malibu house quite accurate, Alexis. How about starting with your first meeting with Scott and telling us how things progressed from there."

Alexis went over everything again, from the first audition to the night Tommy was born. And then on to the night she escaped the burning house with Tommy and never went back.

"How did Scott react to his son's birth?" Jackson asked. "Was he jubilant, detached or somewhere in between?"

"He was ecstatic. He strutted around the birthing room with Tommy in his arms as if a king had been born."

"I thought I read that Tommy was born at home," Meghan said.

"He was, with specially selected and exorbitantly paid doctors and nurses in attendance to ensure that no one knew that Lena had not given birth to their son. Nothing could mar the perfect birth of the Grand Director's first son."

"How about Lena? Was she excited?"

"She was for a few days. After that she went back to the drugs. That hurt, considering I'd given up so much to give her the son that a mere nine months before she'd wanted so badly. I actually took care of Tommy the night he was born and every night thereafter. Not that I didn't love every minute of it."

"Tell me about the birthing room," Meghan said.

"It was just that. A birthing center similar to what you'd find in a hospital, except that it was located in a private wing on the third floor of the house."

"That must have set him back a few mil," Jackson said.

"Money was never an issue with Scott."

"It seems strange for a man who was so proud of having a son to dangle him from a balcony mere months later," Meghan said.

"That was one of the things that never quite added up," Alexis admitted. "Having a son to carry on the family name and bloodline was like an obsession for Scott. He admitted once that was why he'd married Lena Fox."

"Was Lena royalty?" Jackson asked.

"No, but before she became an emaciated addict, she was considered one of the most beautiful women in the world. Men around the globe wrote begging for her hand in marriage. A few of them were royalty. Scott was convinced that with his intellect and talents and her beauty, their son would be the ultimate tribute to his immortality."

"I still don't get why he'd try to kill him," Jackson said. "Was he disappointed in Tommy or Lena?"

"Something happened between the time Tommy was born and the night I tried to protect Tommy with the saber. It seemed to me that Scott began to resent Tommy.

It was as if having a son no longer mattered. Scott never said that out loud, but it was the impression I got."

Jackson wiped a spot of gravy from the front of his shirt. "I've seen that before with powerful men. Their sons usually grow up to hate them."

"But with Scott's growing use of cocaine and his violent mood swings, I was afraid Tommy might not live to grow up."

"I meet the famed director for the first time tomorrow," Meghan said.

"I can't believe he's agreed to talk to a private investigator," Alexis said.

"He didn't. I pulled some strings with an agent friend and she got me an audition with him. I'm trying out for the part of a goddess. Think I can pull that off?"

"I'm sure you can, but be careful," Alexis warned. "I did that once and look where it got me."

"But I ain't birthin' no babies, Miss Scarlet."

The mood grew somber once more as they moved into the complexities of the case and the evidence they'd need to keep Alexis out of jail.

They talked of Scott and Lena at length before Meghan threw out the first surprise of the day.

"I had to dig deep and go back a long way, but I located an arrest record for Scott. Not surprisingly, it was for violence against a woman."

"Was that for abusing one of his wives?" Tague asked.

"No. The complaint was filed by a college girlfriend. But unlike Scott's first two wives, she seems willing to talk to me."

"It's easy to understand why wives one and two aren't squealing on him," Jackson said. "They both draw huge monthly alimony payments, far more than the court ordered. You can bet those payments go with the stipulation that they keep their mouths shut about any of his shortcomings."

Alexis pushed her plate back and leaned forward. "What's the woman's name?"

"Betty Cross, but she was Betty Folse at the time. It was in Illinois, long before Scott had moved to Hollywood or started directing. When I asked her about the complaint she'd filed with the police, she went silent for a few minutes. Then she said, 'Come talk to me.'"

"Sounds promising," Tague said. "I just wish the incident was more recent."

"It's a place to start," Meghan said. "If we can establish that Mr. Marvelous has been known to fly into a rage at any time in his past, it will make Alexis's claims more credible."

"Like I say, monsters don't just pop up overnight," Jackson said. "I'm happy to report that I didn't find any police rap sheets for Alexandra Beretha Cousteau."

"Who?" Tague asked.

"The birth name of our Alexis here."

Alexis nodded. "That's me."

"That's a mouthful," Tague said. "I'll stick with Alexis."

"I also managed to get my hands on copies of your medical files from your alleged emotional breakdown. Two of the three doctors who first examined you found no evidence of psychoses. Scott immediately dismissed their services."

"Scott never told me that. He told me all the doctors agreed that I was a risk to Tommy's safety and threatened me with the possibility of never again being able to spend unsupervised time with him."

"The guy's a bastard," Jackson said. "I can't wait to take him down, but it may take more than a week to dismantle a legend."

Tague stood and retrieved the coffeepot. Once he'd filled everyone's cup, he walked over to Alexis and rested his hands on the back of her chair.

"If you've learned that much in less than twenty-four hours, I don't see why there would be a problem in finishing this in a week."

"That's desk work," Meghan said. "All we've done is get our hands on someone else's paperwork. Field work is a lot more time-consuming."

"Maybe I can help with that," Tague said. "Where does Betty Cross live?"

"In a rural area in southern Illinois," Meghan said. "I've booked a flight into Chicago this afternoon. I'll rent a car when I get there and drive the rest of the way."

"I'm going with you," Tague said. "And don't worry about the flight. If I can't get a company plane on this short notice, I'll charter a flight to fly to the nearest airport to the Crosses' house."

"What about Alexis?" Jackson asked. "Do you need me to stay with her?"

"I'm going with them," Alexis said.

"She and Tommy can stay on the plane with the pilot," Tague agreed.

Alexis excused herself from the group when she heard Tommy's cries. The trip to see Betty Cross offered only a tinge of hope, but it was more than she'd had before. And the medical reports would prove she wasn't the mental case Scott had made her out to be.

But she wouldn't be twiddling her thumbs during the interview with Betty Cross. It was her future and Tom-

my's she was fighting for. She might not get to call all
the shots but she was calling this one.

THE CORNSTALKS WERE well over knee-high and flourish-
ing as they drove the back roads to keep an appointment
with Betty Cross. Tommy was in one of his more play-
ful moods and doing a great job of entertaining Meghan
Sinclair.

"He is so cute," Meghan proclaimed. "Is he always
this happy?"

"Most of the time," Tague said.

"But he can throw a noteworthy tantrum if the situation calls for it," Alexis added.

"Can't we all?" Meghan said.

"He's just turned two," Alexis explained.

"The terrible twos," Meghan said. "It will get worse."

Alexis shifted so that she could see into the backseat.
"Do you have children?"

"No, but I have two young nephews and I remember
well when they went through the scream-and-kick-and-
hold-your-breath phase."

"Is that why you're still single?"

"No. I'm just waiting for the right man, one who *isn't*
afraid of commitment."

"There's the Cross house," Tague announced, inter-
rupting the conversation just as it was getting interesting.

Alexis's anxiety level climbed. Tague had reluctantly
agreed to her talking to Betty Cross with one stipulation: she couldn't take Tommy in with her. If Betty Cross
was even vaguely aware of the kidnapping, she might
suspect Tommy of being Scott's kidnapped son and immediately call 911.

Tague killed the engine and Meghan climbed from the backseat of the rented car.

"Okay, you two," Tague said. "Tommy and I will be back at that last café we passed having ice cream. Call me when you're ready to be picked up."

"Maybe I should stay with Tommy after all," Alexis offered. "You know I'm a terrible actress. Suppose I blow the whole thing?"

Tague reached over and squeezed her hand. "You won't. You're the one who knows Scott best. You should be the one to talk to Betty. Now scoot, you two Hollywood reporters looking for a scoop. And good luck."

Alexis gave Tommy a quick hug before tugging her skirt down and walking toward the yellow farmhouse. She stopped when she saw a man in coveralls standing on the front porch.

"Why do I have the feeling that Scott is standing in the shadows watching me even here in the middle of a cornfield?"

"Because the lying, conniving bastard did a number on you," Meghan said. "I, on the other hand, don't think Scott Hayden would come anywhere near this cornfield unless he was shooting a scene in it. Besides, I think that your luck is about to turn. Betty Cross will be the prize behind door number one."

"I like the way you think."

Betty greeted them and led them to the kitchen. Her husband, Eli, joined them, the skeptical frown he'd worn on the porch still plastered to his weather-roughened face.

Meghan was a marvel at getting people to open up. In minutes, she had Betty offering information without even waiting for the questions.

"Scott and I both grew up in this area, but in separate towns. I didn't meet him until we both started classes at the University of Illinois."

"How long did you know him before you started dating?"

"Just a week or two. It was my freshman year. We sat next to each other in sociology class. One night I invited him to my dorm room to study. It just grew from there."

Betty seemed nervous. Her husband seemed angry. Alexis hoped Betty hadn't traded one monster for another.

"Did he ever talk about his family?" Meghan asked.

"All the time. He was raised by his grandmother. The way he talked, she must have been the meanest woman who ever lived. She used to lock him out of the house when he was just a little kid and sometimes not let him back in until way past dark. She kicked him out for good when he was sixteen."

Scott had told Alexis his parents were both diplomats to Turkey. "Did he do well in school?" she asked.

"Not particularly, but he always blamed his bad grades on the teacher's stupidity. He claimed he'd been tested and fell in the genius range, but I never saw the test scores. He was always talking about making it big and how people were going to look up to him. I mean you'd think he was exiled royalty the way he bragged about himself and what he deserved."

"He was a jerk," Betty's husband said.

"Did you know him, too?" Meghan asked.

"No, but I know how he treated Betty. If I ever see him in person, I'll kick his ass for that. Sorry, but that's how I feel."

"I wouldn't get into a fight with him," Alexis said.

"I hear he has a temper and a bodyguard the size of a small tank."

"How did he treat you?" Meghan asked.

Betty's mouth drew into hard lines. "Like he was better than me. I don't know what I ever saw in him."

"Tell them what he did to you," her husband coaxed. "Don't be ashamed. It was him that did it—not you. People should know what he's really like."

"They should," Alexis agreed.

Betty cast her eyes downward. "I got pregnant. I told Scott about it and he went crazy. I mean like he was madman. He screamed that he didn't want trash like me having his kid. That I'd have to get an abortion or he'd do it for me. Then he banged my head against the wall until I passed out."

"Did you lose the baby?"

"Not then, but I miscarried a few weeks later."

"You must have called the police when he attacked you," Meghan said. "I saw the record of it in the police files."

"I called my dad. He called the police. Then he took his own gun and went out hunting for Scott. Thank God, he didn't find him that night. I think he might have killed him."

"What happened after that?"

"Scott moved out to California. I never heard from him again. Then a few years later, I see him on a TV talk show and he's like some Hollywood big shot."

"I've been telling her for years she ought to call one of those magazines he's always in and tell them what he done to her," Eli said.

"They'd never believe me," Betty said. "I'm a nobody,

and he's famous. Besides, I don't want people around here talking about me."

"What happened to Scott's grandmother?" Meghan asked.

"She died about five years ago. She's buried in that cemetery just off Cougar Road. You'll run into it if you keep going west when you leave here."

Eli must have decided he'd wasted enough time on them. He told them goodbye and left out the back door. A few minutes later, he drove off on his tractor. Betty turned toward the window and watched until he disappeared from sight.

They talked a few more minutes, but Betty just repeated the same things she'd already told them. Alexis called Tague and she and Meghan went out to wait for him on the porch. Betty followed them.

"Are you going to print what I told you about Scott?"

"It could go public at some point," Meghan admitted.

Betty lowered her voice. "That part I told you about getting pregnant with Scott's baby."

"What about it?" Alexis asked.

"It might not be completely true."

There went their smidgen of evidence. The trip to Illinois had likely been for nothing.

"So he didn't hit you and bang your head against the wall?" Meghan asked.

"Oh, he hit me all right. He hurt me bad, but I'm not for certain that was his baby I was pregnant with. I mean, it could have been someone else's. But Scott didn't know that. He just didn't want me having his child. I was kind of glad when someone kidnapped his son. I know that's wrong and I hope that kid is safe, but Scott doesn't deserve kids. He never did."

And he never would. But Alexis seriously doubted Betty's testimony would sway a jury or a judge.

Betty had called it right. She was a nobody. He was famous. That was life in the real world.

Maybe that's why she loved Tague's world so much more than her own.

ALEXIS DELIBERATELY CHOSE a double seat at the back of the plane that didn't allow anyone to sit directly across from her and Tommy. The more she thought about her situation, the angrier she got at Tague, unfair as it might be.

He could have let her and Tommy go on the run again. It wasn't the perfect solution but it was a thousand times better than what would happen if his plans failed.

And what did he know about people like Scott Hayden anyway? If he was shocked that Scott had a mean grandmother, what would he think of her parents? That she was white trash? That she wasn't good enough to have his children the way Scott had thought Betty wasn't good enough to bear his?

Okay, so she was stretching things now, but there were nuggets of truth hiding beneath her irritation. She and Tague lived in different worlds. His was laced with love. Hers was laced with arsenic—or so it had seemed when she was growing up.

But she'd be a good mother to Tommy if the world would just give her a chance.

It was past Tommy's naptime and he fell asleep in minutes. Alexis leaned back and closed her eyes. Tague and Meghan were two rows in front of her, sitting across the aisle from each other. Their voices were easily discernible, their conversation impossible to ignore.

"Both company jets are booked for tomorrow," Tague said. "I had Lambert Inc.'s travel department charter a flight. The plane holds six so there's plenty of room for Jackson to fly back with us."

"How is he getting there?"

"He had a change of plans and he's there now, talking to Lena Fox's older sister. Evidently she welcomed the opportunity to sound off about Scott and about Lena's death."

"Does she think Lena was murdered?"

"Yes, but not by Alexis—or Melinda Ryan as she knows her. She's convinced Scott murdered her, and is furious that now he's using the charge of murder as a publicity scheme to build interest in his new thriller."

"So exactly who's going to California?" Meghan asked.

"You and me. I'm meeting Jackson at his hotel and we're paying a visit to Scott's Malibu estate while Scott's holding auditions in L.A."

"You'll never get inside the gates."

"We'll have an escort," Tague said.

"Lena's sister?"

"Right. Scott had been after her to come out and pick up the rest of Lena's personal belongings. Jackson had her call Scott and tell him she'd be out tomorrow and was bringing a couple of friends to help her haul off the stuff."

"How much stuff is still there?"

"Everything but the furs and jewels that sister dearest rescued before Scott could sell them or give them to another woman."

"So mostly clothes?" Meghan asked.

"A three-closet wardrobe."

"Three closets full of designer dresses, gowns, hand-bags and shoes. And I'll be stuck playacting for Scott. Want to trade places?"

"Not unless the role you're auditioning for is cowboy-without-a-horse, because that's what I feel like now."

"Durk always said you and Damien were cowboys to the core."

"And he's a cowboy at heart," Tague said.

"Which would indicate he had a heart."

Alexis opened her eyes, her curiosity piqued by Meghan's tone and words. She'd love to know what had happened between Meghan and Tague's brother Durk. There had to be a story there and her guess was Meghan wasn't over him yet.

If Durk was anything like Tague, she could under-stand that. Her irritation with Tague had dropped dras-tically since they'd boarded the plane. She had no right to complain. Her problems had taken over his life and still he searched for ways to do more.

But going to Scott's Malibu estate was a terrible and extremely dangerous idea. If Scott found out that Tague was involved with Alexis, he'd explode. She had to find a way to make Tague change his mind.

MEGHAN HAD TAKEN her own car from the Austin airport, leaving Tague, Alexis and Tommy to drive home to-gether. Tague had tried to make conversation with Alexis but she'd withdrawn into a shell he couldn't seem to crack.

He turned onto the winding, wooded road that led to the camp. "I'm a guy, Alexis. You'll have to tell me what I've done wrong if you want me to fix it. I'll never figure it out on my own."

She turned to face him. "Okay. I'll tell you what's wrong. You keep underestimating Scott. You act like spying on him at his house is as safe as walking to the horse barn back at the Bent Pine Ranch."

"I take it you overheard my conversation with Meghan?"

"You weren't exactly whispering."

"Why should I? I have nothing to hide. Maybe the real problem is that you keep underestimating *me*. You expect me to cower in fear while we wait for Scott to make the next move."

"I expect you to stay safe, Tague. I expect you not to go looking to get your head bashed in. I expect you to…"

"Go ahead. Say it. You expect me to what?"

"To stay alive. I don't want to lose you to a madman, Tague." Fear edged her voice.

Tague pulled off on the shoulder of the road and let the truck roll to a stop. Then he put his seat back as far as it would go, reached for Alexis and pulled her into his arms.

"I don't want to lose you, either, Alexis. I can't imagine that I'd ever want to let you go."

Their lips met in a heated wave of passion that stole his breath and sent desire coursing through every part of his body. Thoughts of reality and danger and restraint vanished.

There was nothing but the sweet taste of her on his tongue and the feel of her body pressing against his.

"Kiss. Kiss. Kiss."

Tommy's ill-timed childish mocking jerked him back to his senses. He pulled away but trailed his fingertips along Alexis's arm until their hands clasped.

"I promise you that I'm not taking any of this lightly,

Alexis. It's my nature to joke and keep things light. It works for me. So does going at a problem full speed ahead. But I don't ride a horse to the edge of a cliff and then yell *whoa* or face a grizzly with a pellet gun.

"I plan to come home from California in one piece and I'll tell you all about it over dinner tomorrow night."

"I could go with you," Alexis said.

"And be arrested the second someone on the staff recognizes you. I don't see how that can help any of us. Now, let's go back to the camp. Damien and Emma will be arriving soon and I can't wait for you all to meet each other."

"A second cowboy to feed," she teased.

"Yee-haw, ride the horsey," Tommy sang out of the blue.

"Better make that three cowboys," Tague said. His cell phone jangled. He pulled it from his pocket and checked the caller ID. "It's Hampton," he said.

"Don't answer. It will be bad news."

He answered anyway.

And the news was bad.

Chapter Thirteen

"Good news and bad," Hampton said, "unless you're Alexis Beranger. In that case, it's all bad."

"I hate to hear that. She seemed like a nice lady. But I'm not sure why you're calling me about her problems."

"I just thought you'd be interested in hearing that we've ID'd the two dead guys that were found in her apartment."

"Who are they?"

"Harvey Epstein and Galen Barresi."

"Never heard of them," Tague said, still acting nonchalant. "What's their relationship to Alexis?"

"They're friends of the carjacker. Good friends, as in the kind you call on when it's payback time."

"So you think they went there to attack Alexis?"

"They're not the kind of guys who drop by to paint your apartment."

He kept his voice low while Alexis engaged Tommy in a noisy action song about bears going over a mountain. "Who killed them? Rival gang members?"

"Could be, but with the new information I have about Alexis Beranger, I'd say anything's possible."

"Are you going to say what that new information is or wait for me to guess?"

"I don't think you'd have to guess, Tague. I think you were probably the first one to figure out that Alexis Beranger isn't Alexis Beranger."

"You lost me, Detective. Want to back up a step? If she's not Alexis Beranger, who is she?"

"Melinda Ryan Hayden, better known as the wife who kidnapped Scott Jeffery Hayden's son."

"No way. She seemed so nice. I insisted she spend the night at my house. I guess I should call Mother and tell her to check for missing jewelry."

"Don't put me on, Tague. Aiding a known felon is a serious crime. I'm not saying you have her with you or anything like that, but if you know where she is, you need to come clean now."

"What would happen to her if I did?"

"She'd go to jail and the kid would be returned to his father. That's where he rightfully belongs."

"It would seem that way," Tague agreed. "Unless there are extenuating circumstances."

"There are no extenuating circumstances that justify kidnapping. But that may not even be Melinda Ryan's biggest problem."

"There's more?"

"One of her two deceased drop-by visitors arrived with a bottle of acid."

"And then used it on a guy meaner than he was and didn't live to tell about it," Tague said. "How does that make things more dangerous for Alexis?"

"There is no Alexis. I'm just saying if the Death Knights find Melinda Ryan before I do, she might end up dead."

"If I hear from her, I'll advise her to turn herself in."

"If you hear from her, find out where she is and call me. And then butt out of it. You're not a police officer."

"Exactly. So how did you discover Alexis's true identity?"

"Fingerprints were collected from her car. All of them went through the system, hers as well as Booker Dell Collins's. He's been charged with carjacking and attempted kidnapping. There's an APB out all over Texas for Melinda's arrest."

"Then I'm sure you'll find her soon."

"I hope we do—for her sake and the kid's."

"Did you get prints from the house so that you can identify the head bashers?"

"All I can tell you is that there were two men who walked away from the apartment. From the evidence we found, we know that one of them was big enough to be a linebacker for the Cowboys. You may be tough, Tague, but you don't want to mess with him."

Not without a gun.

As MUCH AS Alexis wanted to hear everything Hampton had told Tague, she didn't want Tommy exposed to it. Once back at the lodge, she quickly settled Tommy in the living room floor with his blocks and minicars. Then she joined Tague in the kitchen.

"I made a pot of coffee," he said. "Would you like a cup?"

"I'd like something stronger—a lot stronger. Something that will burn all the way down my throat and I'll feel it when it hits my stomach."

Tague poured a shot of whiskey and set the glass in front of her.

"Are you going to make me drink alone?"

"I am tonight," he said. "I want to be totally lucid when I explain everything to Damien. He has a good head for problem solving, and I respect his opinion. I don't always follow it, but I respect it."

Hopefully Damien had the good sense to tell Tague to stay away from Scott and his estate.

She sipped the whiskey and relished the burn. "What did I miss by singing through your end of the conversation with Detective Hampton?"

He leaned back in his chair. "The victims were members of the Death Knights. They don't know who killed them, except that one of the men was really big."

"I know who killed them. It was Scott and his bodyguard."

"That's pure speculation."

"That's a fact," Alexis said. "The big man was Bronco. His hands and feet are gigantic. His shirts could be used for a tent. And it would be just like Scott to show up with the baseball bat. He was there to have me arrested, but when he ran into the Death Knights, he killed them."

"They may have attacked him first," Tague said. "They arrived bearing gifts—like a bottle of acid, so they definitely weren't making a friendly call."

She shuddered at the thought of acid thrown into her face. It would be even worse had it touched Tommy's tender skin.

She downed the rest of the whiskey in one gulp. "I've made such a mess of things. It's hard to believe this all started with my wanting to help Lena and Scott have a baby. Now Lena's dead. Scott's gone mad. And I can't give Tommy any kind of continuity or even keep him safe."

"And none of that is your fault." Tague reached across the table and laid his hands over hers. "We'll get through this, Alexis. It takes time, but at least we're working on a solution now. If you'd kept running, things would have only gotten worse."

"Not if I'd never been caught."

"You need a home, a real home and possessions that you don't have to limit to what will fit in a couple of monstrous suitcases and some paper bags."

"How long do you think it will be before Hampton shows up here looking for me? My real home will be a jail cell. And Tommy's will be living with a monster."

"I'm hoping for a few more days, but even if Hampton or any officer of the law shows up and arrests you, it will just be a temporary setback. I'll keep working until I find a way to prove you didn't kill Lena or start a fire, or do anything worse than protect the life of the boy you gave birth to."

"Easy for you to say, but I'm telling you that Scott will make sure I stay in jail until I rot."

"I hate to say this, Alexis, but I don't think Scott has any intention of having you arrested."

"Of course he does," she protested. "Why else would he have been at my house?"

"If he'd planned to involve the police, he would have done so by now. He'd have given them your phone number and told them how to find you instead of showing up there with his pet giant. I think he called you because he wanted you to run."

"Why would he want me to...?"

The truth finally hit home. "He wanted me to run so that he could kill me and make it look like he'd done it to rescue his son."

"That's the only thing that makes sense," Tague said. "Only somehow he lost track of you when you left in my truck."

"And when he went back to my apartment to see if he could get a clue to help him figure out where I'd gone, he ran into the Death Knight members and killed them. And just because he directs movies and makes millions for doing it, he'll likely never go to jail for any of that or for setting fire to his own house with people inside."

Alexis heard a car engine and then the slamming of car doors.

Tague rushed to the window and peeked through the slants of the blind. "It's Damien and Emma," he said. "Now that Damien's on our team, the opposition doesn't have a chance.

"Then send Damien to California."

If Tague heard her, he ignored the comment in his rush to welcome two more Lamberts to the hunting camp.

She only hoped that Scott and Bronco weren't the next visitors in line.

"How in the world did you get into a mess like this?"

"Your fault," Tague said. "I went into town to pick up the saddle you had made for Emma and trouble found me."

"I suppose the fact that trouble came in a beautiful package had nothing to do with it?"

"It might have added a bit to the lure."

"So fill me in on all the details before I fall asleep. I'm still living on Paris time."

Tague leaned back in the yard chair and looked up at

the stars. "Okay, but listen close. This may be the most
bizarre tale you've ever heard."

"More bizarre than Emma's being kidnapped by an
arms dealer and living in captivity for months before
escaping?"

"Let's just say it's in that same horror genre."

An hour later they'd covered it all, and no easy solu-
tions had jumped out at them.

"Let me sleep on it," Damien said. "We'll talk again
in the morning."

"Okay, but I'm counting on you to stay here with
Alexis and Tommy tomorrow."

"I'd rather make the California run with you."

"But I need you here in case Detective Hampton
shows up or sends someone in law enforcement from
this area to make an arrest. I don't want Alexis to try
anything foolish and I damn sure don't want her to get
the chance to go on the run again. Not with Scott out
to kill her."

"You can count on me."

"I know. It's good to have you here, bro. Really good."

"That's what brothers are for."

ALEXIS HAD JUST turned off her lamp and snuggled beneath the sheet when she heard the soft tapping at her
door. She switched the light back on and smoothed the
top of her pink pajamas as she sat up in bed.

"Come in."

Tague stuck his head inside the bedroom. "Mind if I
come in for a minute?"

"Of course not. Is something wrong?"

"I just wanted to make sure you were okay."

"As okay as I'm going to get under the circumstances."

He walked over and sat down on the other side of her bed.

She ached to reach out and touch him, the way she always did when he was near. But touch might lead to a kiss, and this time Tommy was asleep in the next room. He wouldn't be there to bring her back to reality before she went too far.

"What do you think of Damien and Emma?" he asked.

"I liked them. Damien reminds me of you."

"And Emma?"

"She's terrific. I think if things were different we could become very good friends. We didn't get to talk much, but she told me a bit of the terrifying ordeal she went through and how Damien had saved her life."

Tague leaned back against the headboard and pulled his stockinged feet to the top of the covers. "You never talk about your family, Alexis. Why is that?"

"They're not around."

"Where are they?"

"My mother could be anywhere. My father is probably just getting home from work and dragging himself to bed."

"There must be more to tell me about them than that."

"They're the opposite of your family in every way. Does that suffice?"

"If it's all you want to say about them, I guess it has to suffice."

"I didn't grow up rich the way you did, Tague. We weren't exactly poor, either. I mean I didn't go wanting for food or clothes or material things."

"What about love and happiness?"

"For the most part, I missed out on those," she admitted. She pulled up her legs and wrapped her arms around her knees. There really was no reason not to tell Tague about her family. She was who she was.

"My mother was a singer with a jazz band. She was away almost every night and sleeping in when I left for school in the morning. When our paths crossed, it was for her to remind me to do my homework or clean up my room."

"That must have been tough on you."

"I got used to it."

"How did your father feel about her being gone all the time?"

"I'm not sure he even noticed. He was a workaholic. He came home late, grabbed a sandwich or some soup and ate in front of the TV. Half the time he fell asleep on the sofa with the plate still in his hand."

"Are they still together?"

"No, they divorced when I was twelve. My mother moved in with the drummer. I seldom saw her after that. And Dad worked even later. I quit school midway through my senior year of high school and moved to California. People kept saying I was pretty enough to be in the movies and I foolishly believed that was all it took to become a star."

"No wonder you were taken in by the likes of Scott Hayden."

"That was a few years and a dozen B-rated movies later. By then I was totally frustrated and weary of struggling to make a living by waitressing between auditions and movie roles that barely covered my rent."

"And then you received an invitation to move into

Scott Hayden's Malibu beach house. I can see how you'd be thrilled at an opportunity like that."

"From barely scraping by to living in a mansion. I thought I'd arrived. Turned out I had arrived in hell. My only salvation was Tommy. He became my life. He still is."

"I can tell, but you're young. You have plenty of time to make a new life for you and Tommy when this is over."

"I'm twenty-five," she said. "That's not so terribly young."

"It's a year younger than I am."

"Then you might be too old for me," she teased.

"Let's just see about that."

The next thing she knew she was in his arms. Her heart was racing. Her insides rolled as if she were on a roller coaster. And the need inside just wouldn't quit.

She melted into his kiss and the nightmare that had become her life dissolved into a passion-filled fantasy.

Chapter Fourteen

Tague kissed her until her lips grew numb and the rest of her became a raging fire. His fingers fumbled with the buttons on her pajamas. As the fabric fell away his hands cupped her breasts and his thumbs raked across her nipples.

She trembled with passion and arched toward him. The hardness of his erection pressed against her and she could feel the hot dampness in the triangle of her desire.

"Is something wrong?" Tague asked. "Did I hurt you?"

"You did nothing wrong, Tague Lambert. You do everything right."

"Then I'm rushing you?"

"Something like that. Only it's not you. It's me. For most of my adult life, I've let life control me. I don't want to do that anymore. I want to make decisions and take back control of my life."

"And you've decided you don't want me?"

"I want you. I want you more than I've ever wanted anyone in my life, but I don't want us to just happen because of the situation we're in. I don't want the first time we make love to be framed by my fear of Scott. I only want it to be about us. I hope you can understand."

"I don't understand, but I accept it."

"You don't understand because you've always been in charge of your life. Thanks to you, I'm just learning how."

"Then I may have created a monster."

He kissed her again, sweetly this time, like velvet brushing against her kiss-swollen lips.

The words "I love you" sang inside her, but she didn't say them out loud. Like making love, that could wait until she held her own future and the assurance of tomorrow in her hands.

If she never did, then Tague would move on without her. And she'd go back to being Alexandra Cousteau, a woman who'd never found a place where she belonged.

SCOTT JEFFERY HAYDEN's Malibu beach estate felt more like a cold stone fortress than a home. Elaborate decorations, modern furniture that looked like it was designed in a carnival house of mirrors and enough marble to open a mine.

Tague stood in the doorway of a formal dining room that was as long as most people's houses. "Scott must throw some wingdinger dinner parties in this room."

"He does, about twice a year. The rest of the time this room is a morgue for aging china patterns. But you ain't seen nothing yet," Lena's sister Gabrielle promised as she led them to the next room.

Gabrielle was attractive, smartly dressed and Tague figured her to be in her mid-fifties or thereabouts. She'd offered the tour of the property, and he and Jackson had jumped at the chance for the guided excursion through the life and times of Scott Jeffery Hayden.

For the most part the household staff had stayed clear

of them, but Tague had the feeling they were keeping an eye on them from shadowed hiding spots. Gabrielle didn't seem the least bit concerned about them.

They entered another rectangular room, this one narrower and shorter than the dining room, but no less pretentious. The chandelier would have provided adequate lighting for the Texan's football game on a dark, foggy night.

"This must be the awards gallery," Jackson said. "Look at all the little statues, plaques and quaint doll-sized director's chairs lined up to play homage to the great man himself."

"Not to mention the framed certificates that cover the walls," Gabrielle said. "Have you ever seen anything so egotistical in your life?"

"I take it you aren't a fan of Scott," Tague said.

"I've never seen Scott's work. I seldom go to movies and when I do, I don't want any reminders of the pompous bastard who made an addict of my sister and then killed her."

"Do you really think Scott killed your sister?"

"I know he did and I finally convinced the D.A. to reopen the case."

"Why are you so convinced it was murder?"

"Because she told me the morning she died that she feared for her life. Scott had apparently learned of some secret that she'd kept from him and he was furious."

"Did she tell anyone else that?"

"I doubt it, but she shouldn't have had to. I'm her sister. Telling me should have been enough."

"What did you do to protect her?"

"Not one darn thing. She poured out her heart to me but I thought it was just the drugs talking. She came to me and I did nothing to help. Now I have to live with that, but I could live better if I knew Scott was paying for her death with his life."

"How do you think he killed her?"

"He forced the drugs through her veins. She never gave herself injections. She took pills and far too many of them, but never injections."

"Did you tell that to the investigating cops when she died?"

"Yes and again when our new D.A. took office and I persuaded him to take another look at the evidence. And then the cops immediately turned all their focus toward Melinda."

"Then you don't buy that Alexis had anything to do with her death?" Tague asked.

"Alexis? Hardly. She wouldn't hurt a fly. I'm glad she left with Tommy. I hope the cops never find her. Tommy's much better off with her than he would be with his rabid father."

Gabrielle didn't mince words. Honest indignation. Tague preferred that over insincere niceties any day.

"I suppose we should go to Lena's room now and pack a few things," Gabrielle said. "I'm sure my ex-brother-in-law will question the staff tonight about how much time I spent here and how many boxes I lugged from the house."

"But he must trust you if he gives you the run of the place," Jackson said.

"Scott doesn't trust anyone. Dishonest men never do. It's just that he knows he has nothing I want. Lena was a star long before she met him. She made sure I had ample money to live on the rest of my life without working a day—if that's what I chose to do."

"Do you work?" Jackson asked.

"I'm a writer, a one-book wonder, or at least I will be when I've finished the book." She put a finger to her lip as if to hush them. "I'll tell you all about it when there are no curious ears hiding in the hallway.

"There's one more room you're sure to enjoy. Lena always called it the Wives' Bizarre Bazaar, similar to the trophy room but with the trophies being the parade of wives. Pick a wife and learn all about that period of Scott's life."

The room set at the end of a long hallway was circular with panels of solid glass that offered a gorgeous view of the ocean. In between the glass were wooden panels of equal size, each one showcasing a portrait of one of Scott's four wives.

"Lena's theory was that each wife represented a different phase in Scott's career. This is Angelique, wife number one."

"She's a looker," Jackson said. "Which phase is she?"

"The struggling phase. Scott needed money to fund the projects that would eventually make him one of the most sought-after directors in Hollywood. Angelique was an heiress. He chose well."

"And wife number two?" Tague asked as he stepped to the next panel."

"Barbara. Scott was well on his way to the top. He wanted excitement and pizzazz and sex. Barbara was his sex goddess."

"That's the wife I'm looking for," Jackson said.

Next was Lena. She had been a fabulous-looking woman when her portrait was painted. "Lena must have been chosen for the parenthood period of life," Tague said.

"That's exactly what she said. Scott had more money than he could spend. He had every manly toy money could buy, but the one thing he couldn't buy was a son."

Tague figured Lena had oversimplified the wives issue, but she probably wasn't totally off target.

"And then there's Alexis," Jackson said. "What was she, the need-a-mommy-for-my-kid phase?"

"Indeed not. Everyone who ever saw Alexis and Scott together knew what Alexis represented. She was the happiness that had always eluded him. She was the one woman he truly loved."

Tague got that. It was hard to imagine anyone spending a lot of time with her and not falling in love with her. But she hadn't loved Scott back and he hadn't been able to bear the rejection.

Finally, they made it back to Lena's suite. Gabrielle pointed to a sitting area. "Take a seat. I have something shocking to show you, or at least it shocked me."

She reached into her oversize handbag and took out a brown envelope. "This came to me as a registered letter the day of the funeral. Afraid that it would be too painful to read, I kept it locked in a bureau drawer for six weeks. Since then, I've had it in my safety deposit box." She handed the envelope to Tague.

The letter inside was printed but hand signed by a Dr. William Reese. Scott read the letter through twice and then handed it to Jackson.

"Son of a bitch," Jackson said. "Pardon my French, but this is the last thing I expected. All the talk of Lena not being able to have a baby and it turns out Scott is sterile."

Tague took the letter from Jackson and returned it to the envelope. "If Scott's not Tommy's father, who is?"

"I honestly have no idea," Gabrielle said. "After reading that, I'm not even sure that Lena was the mother. Perhaps Alexis was pregnant by some other man and Scott just wanted a son so badly he concocted the whole in vitro fertilization story. He gave Alexis free room and board. She gave him the son he and Lena couldn't have. And then he fell in love with her."

This was totally blowing Tague's mind. Lena spun an interesting scenario, but he couldn't believe that Alexis was still lying to him. He'd accepted that she lied in the beginning, but not now. Not when they'd become so close.

He had to know the truth, but he wouldn't confront her until he did.

"May I take the letter with me?" Tague asked.

"Not that one. It's the original, but I made a copy for you. There's also a legal form that I think might interest you." She reached back into her handbag and handed him a notarized form. This was signed by both Lena and Scott and two witnesses whose names he didn't recognize.

The form stated that if anything happened to keep Lena and Scott from taking care of Tommy, Melinda Ryan was to be named as legal guardian.

"I can't believe Scott signed this," he said.

"Remember, that was when he was planning on making her his wife and before she openly rejected him."

But this form would work against Alexis. It gave her a motive to want both Lena and Scott dead so that she'd have sole custody of Tommy. But if Tommy were her child, she could have just had DNA testing done and proven that.

Tague could do nothing but speculate now. He needed facts.

Neither he nor Jackson stayed around to haul out clothes. There were far more important things to take care of, starting with Dr. Reese.

"THE QUICKEST WAY to get at the truth is likely the old-fashioned paper trail," Jackson said as they drove away from Scott's mansion. "I already have Scott's banking records for the month Alexis would have gotten pregnant."

"How did you get that?"

"Don't ask. You don't want to know. Pull in at that coffee shop over there. They probably have wireless. I need to bring up my files."

It only took a few minutes to discover that a huge check had been written to a fertility clinic in Beverly Hills for the month in question. They found a phone number for the clinic online, but it was no longer in business.

Within another thirty minutes, Jackson and Tague had worked together to get the full scoop. The clinic had been closed when the two doctors who'd operated it had been arrested for selling "designer sperm" from donors who believed they were anonymous.

"What exactly is 'designer sperm'?" Tague asked.

"It's when a person goes in with a list of qualities they specifically want in the sperm they're buying. For example, you may want a child who's an intellectual or one with unusual prowess in athletic fields or with a specific talent. The sperm bank gets you what you want, or at least claim to for a price that's much higher than the normal price."

"Is that illegal?"

"Not normally, but in this case the sperm bank was paying large sums of money for sperm from their chosen donors. The donors were assured they would remain anonymous, but in some cases where the people were well-known, the clinic was using their name to get even higher bucks."

"In that case I'm sure Scott bought the best sperm available for his perfect son."

"Yes," Jackson said, "but did he use Lena's egg? Or is Alexis the real biological mother?"

"I guess that is the conundrum," Tague said.

"I might be able to get my hands on the clinic's records and find out for you."

"No," Tague said. "I'm through investigating Alexis. Either we trust each other to tell the truth or there is no point in pursuing it. Let's meet up with Meghan and fly home."

GERALD HAMPTON HAD someone watching the turnoff road to Bent Pine Ranch day and night. He knew for a fact that Tague Lambert had not been back to the ranch since the morning he'd supposedly driven Melinda Ryan to rent a car.

No one in the Dallas area had rented a car to a person name Alexis Beranger. Even more telling was the fact that no employee at any car agency remembered seeing a woman that matched her description.

He would have never thought a Lambert would jump in on the side of a kidnapper, but he was starting to believe that Tague had done just that. Not just helped her escape, which would be bad enough. But he was protecting her, hiding her from the law.

He could have taken her anywhere. He definitely had the means. But Hampton suspected he was still in the area. All he had to do was figure out where a Lambert would go if they were looking for isolation and seclusion.

How difficult could that be?

MEGHAN CROSSED HER legs, giving Scott Hayden a glimpse of thigh that went almost to the crotch of her red thong panties. She'd used her most feminine wiles at the audition and won the role she was after—a dinner date with the legendary Scott Jeffery Hayden.

It didn't take long to figure out he had the morals of an alley cat. But so far she'd gotten no new information to help Alexis's case.

He ordered the second round of drinks for them. She'd managed to sip a little and pour the rest in his glass when he wasn't looking. He was getting loaded fast, but he had a driver waiting for him in a limo outside, so his getting drunk wouldn't cause a wreck.

"Go home with me tonight and I can show you a good time," Scott said. "Hell, spend the week. You can sleep in a different bedroom every night if you want."

She reached over and rubbed his thigh. "What if I just want to sleep in the one you're in?"

"In that case there might be a little diamond trinket served with your coffee one morning."

She rubbed a little harder and let her fingers slip between his thighs. "I thought you were married."

"I thought I was, too. Turns out we're both wrong." He laughed too loudly and too hard for it not to be faked. Then he leaned over and whispered a sweet nothing in her ear that turned out to be something big.

"I don't believe you," she said. "You're just trying to get me in your bed."

"I got the proof right here."

"Let me see it," she cooed.

He did, and it was the real thing.

After that, she couldn't get out of the restaurant and away from Scott fast enough. She started to call Tague on the way to the airport to give him the news. She changed her mind on the first ring.

Alexis should be the one to give him news like this.

Chapter Fifteen

It was four in the morning before Tague made it back to the hunting camp. He'd slept a few hours on the flight back from California but he'd been awake long enough to make some major decisions.

He had a list of some of the country's best defense attorneys ready to start calling after breakfast. He would put together a dream team, give them all the information they'd gathered so far and then he'd let them call the shots.

They could even go with Alexis to turn herself in. That was his best offer. That was his only offer.

She couldn't go on evading arrest. He couldn't continue to help her do it. It wasn't fair to anyone.

He fell asleep on the sofa and didn't stir until after eight the next morning. By that time the odors of fresh brewed coffee and frying bacon permeated the house.

When he reached the kitchen, Damien pushed a mug of coffee into his hand. "You look terrible, bro. What time did you get in last night?"

"I didn't. I got in this morning. What did you do with the women?"

"They went for a walk, but I told them to stay nearby.

Tommy's with them, so they probably won't make it past the first grasshopper."

"It does take him a long time to get from point A to point B," Tague said."

"Yeah. Cute kid. I guess I've just never pictured you as a father."

"I'm not a father."

"I've seen the way you and Alexis look at each other. Looks like the look of love to me. And I should know. I'm still under the spell myself."

"Yes, but you know what you've got. I'm still trying to figure it out. And even if I had it figured out, it could all change after today."

"Want to talk about it?" Damien asked.

"Yeah. I'd like to run it by you and then I'll go find Alexis and run it by her. But my mind's made up. You and Emma can drive back to the ranch today."

He explained the new developments and the plan to Damien. Then he went in search of Alexis.

He thought he'd feel a tinge of relief that the decision had been made, but all he felt was emptiness down clear to his soul.

ALEXIS SNUGGLED INTO the Adirondack chair, then kicked out of her sandals and pulled her feet in with her.

"I have news," she said. "Super news."

"Let's hear it," Tague said.

"Maybe I should hear yours first. You look as if you need to get it off your chest and then I can cheer you up with mine."

"That's a deal." He started with the meeting with Gabrielle. When he got to the part about Scott being sterile, Alexis threw her hands in the air.

"So that lying, manipulating Scott Hayden was sterile and he let Lena and me believe that I was carrying their baby."

"Lena had to know the truth," Tague said. "She had the original letter from the doctor."

"I am surprised that she had the letter in her possession," Alexis said. "I'm shocked that he even showed it to her."

"She had the original," Tague said. "It had been mailed directly to her."

They both grew silent for a few moments.

"That explains it all," Tague said, as the puzzle pieces seemed to fall together in his mind. "It all revolves around Scott's finding out he was sterile. The change in Scott's feelings about Tommy so soon after his birth, the resentment and maybe even Lena's death."

"Exactly," Alexis said, keying in to what he was asserting. "Lena had the tests run and then she intercepted the letter so that Scott didn't find out he was sterile until after Tommy was born."

"When he did, his jubilation nose-dived. His feelings changed toward the boy and no doubt toward Lena," Tague said. "He'd been duped."

Alexis nodded. "That would have angered him enough that he might have killed Lena."

"Lena's sister thinks he killed her by shooting her full of drugs."

"If there were injections involved, he'd have had to give them," Alexis said. "Lena was deathly afraid of needles. Of course, that means he found out the truth about Tommy's parentage shortly after his birth."

"On the day that Lena called her sister and said that Scott was going to kill her."

"So now we don't know who Tommy's father is," Alexis said. "Not that it matters. It can't be as bad as having Scott's genes. What else did you learn?"

He felt a rush of relief that she hadn't lied to him about Tommy's birth, but the weight refused to lift from his mind.

"Gabrielle has notarized paperwork that states that in the event that neither Lena nor Scott is alive or physically able to take care of Tommy, that you become his guardian."

"Thank God for Lena. I'm sure she saw to that. She knew how much I loved her son."

Tague didn't bring up the concern that the arrangement gave Alexis motive to kill both Lena and Scott. The defense attorneys would be better able to deal with that. He told her the rest, that while he'd keep the investigators working as long as needed, they would have to go with the attorneys' recommendations.

She stood, her shoulders drooping, her eyes downcast. "It didn't have to be this way. You could have just let me take Tommy and run."

"We'll prove your innocence," he said. "I'm getting the best lawyers money can buy."

She turned to walk away.

"I thought you had news," he said. "Let's hear it."

"It doesn't really matter anymore."

He wanted to go after her, but she wouldn't want his touch. She'd likely never want it again. He took his phone and started making calls to attorneys. Three hours later he had his dream team in place.

SCOTT HAD JUST climbed from his swimming pool when his cell phone started vibrating across the deck. He checked the caller ID, then picked up the phone and answered. "This had better be good. If not, consider yourself off the payroll."

"I know where you can find Melinda."

DAMIEN AND EMMA had left for the ranch right after breakfast. Emma couldn't wait to get home to Belle.

Alexis had spent the rest of the day with Tommy, talking to him, singing with him, playing games, teaching him things, telling him she loved him. This could be her last full day with him before the authorities took him away. Her heart was breaking.

So was Tague's. He was beginning to second-guess every decision he'd made. But deep in his heart, he knew he'd done the only thing he could do. If he let her run, Scott would find her and kill her. At least this way she'd stay alive and have a chance of clearing her name.

In fact, he'd never give up until she was completely exonerated. But this might be his last night with Alexis and she didn't want him anywhere near her. She'd gone to bed when Tommy had and closed her door.

He went to his bedroom, took a shower and then pulled on a clean pair of jeans. Without bothering to snap them, he started back to the kitchen. Tonight he was the one who needed the whiskey—straight up.

The floorboards in the hallway creaked beneath his feet, but there was another sound as well. Someone was rattling the back door. He grabbed his pistol and went to see what the devil was going on.

He looked out the back door but saw no one. He went back for his gun and stepped onto the back steps. He

caught only a glimpse of the giant fist as it came crashing down on the back of his skull. He saw the steps fly
up to meet him and then everything went black.

Chapter Sixteen

Alexis was lying in her bed wide-awake and staring at the ceiling when she heard the crash. She jumped to the floor and took off running. Halfway down the hall, she heard Scott's voice barking orders.

Fear pummeled her so hard and fast that the narrow hallway began to spin. She fell against the wall and leaned there just long enough to regain her balance.

She needed a weapon. This was a hunting camp. There should be guns, but she hadn't seen one except for the antiques on the wall. They must have kept the hunting guns locked away or brought them with them when they came. There was no saber, no hunting knife, at least not here in the hall.

Footsteps started coming toward her. She reached up and yanked a framed picture from the wall. She banged it as hard as she could against the floor. The glass shattered and she managed to retrieve a jagged piece of it just as Scott stepped into view.

"Fancy meeting you here," he said. "And ready to fight me and Bronco off with that tiny shard of glass."

"What do you want with me, Scott?"

"My son, for starters."

"Tommy's not your son. You have no son and you never will. God saw to that."

"But the world doesn't know that." He kicked Alexis back to the floor with a heavy boot to her face. Blood splattered from her nose.

She reeled in pain, then struggled to focus as fear and anger surged inside her. "Why are you here, Scott? You don't want me. You don't want Tommy. So why chase us down as if we were roaches you had to stomp?"

"Because you killed Lena and now you have to die for the crime."

"I didn't kill her. You did."

"You're the madwoman. Of course you killed her. If you don't believe me, just ask the cops. And once you turn up dead, you won't even be able to mount a defense."

"They'll know you killed me."

"That's impossible. I'm at home in Malibu. My housekeeper and my driver will vouch for that."

"If they do, it's only because you're holding something over their heads. Where's Tague?" she demanded.

"Not to worry, my dear. He'll be at your performance. Bronco just has to get him ready first."

"There is no performance. Think about what you're doing, Scott. All the things you've accomplished will be for nothing if you kill us in cold blood. All anyone will ever remember of you is that you're a murderer."

"They'll never connect me to this. It's the carjacker's friends who tracked you down. What a shame."

"You hired that thug to carjack me, didn't you? You were behind everything. I should have known."

She struggled to her feet. Scott shoved her against

the wall and pushed his body against hers, holding her hands over her head so that she couldn't break away.

"It's called genius, my sweet. Hiring a thug already known by the cops to kidnap and kill you. But it's much better this way. Now his friends will get the blame but I'll get the pleasure of seeing you perform one last time before you die, sweet Melinda."

He put his lips on hers. She bit down hard on his bottom lip.

He bit back and she cried out in pain. Fighting him was useless. His strength was overpowering.

"Such a spitfire," Scott said, his voice gritty with fury. "I loved that about you. I loved everything about you, Melinda, but you ruined it all."

"Where's Tague?" she demanded again. "Have you hurt him?"

"Yes, he's most definitely hurt. But I do hope he's not dead. I'd so hate for him to miss the show. Now we really should get started."

Alexis shuddered. This wasn't a fit of rage. This time Scott was as cold and as calculating as he'd ever been when directing a movie. Maybe he'd always balanced precariously on the edge between genius and madness.

If she didn't do something fast, he'd kill her. For all she knew Tague might already be dead. The possibility was like a knife in her heart.

Scott took a step toward her. She plunged at him with the jagged fragment of glass. He caught her arm and spun her around, twisting both arms around her back and forcing her to the floor.

"Get in here, Bronco. We don't have all night. The show must go on."

Bronco stepped into the hallway behind Scott. Blood

dripped from his chin and the front of his shirt. But not his blood. There wasn't a scratch on him. The blood had to be Tague's. She gagged on the bile that gurgled into her throat.

"Is our audience ready?"

Bronco nodded, but didn't speak.

"Then carry the lovely Melinda Ryan to wardrobe."

Bronco threw her over his shoulders like a sack of potatoes. When she tried to kick free, he squeezed so tight that she was afraid he'd cracked a lung. Pain ripped through her and she struggled to breathe.

Bronco sat her down in a chair opposite the sofa. Tague was propped up against two large throw pillows in a chair nearest the door, but his eyes were closed and he wasn't moving. Blood soaked his shirt.

"Put this on, Melinda. And make it quick. If you dawdle, I'll put it on you, and you know how wicked my hands can be."

It was the same black negligee she'd worn at her callback audition for him, or at least one very similar.

"Do you remember your lines, Melinda? A good actress always remembers her lines."

Weirdly, she did remember them. Her voice shook as she started to recite them. She had to buy time and find a way to escape. She had to save Tague. She had to get Tommy away from the madman before they all ended up dead.

"The lines, Melinda. Say them or I have Bronco hit Tague again."

Her voice quaked as she began reciting. "'I know you're in here. I know you're watching me. I can't see you, but I hear your breathing.'"

"You're doing much, much better this time, Alexis. I

actually see and hear your fear. Keep going. Convince me you can do it."

"'Why are you stalking me? Is it because I'm blind? Is it that you're so disgustingly ugly that no other woman will let you near her?'"

"Keep going. The last few lines are the best."

Tague's head moved ever so slightly. Ridiculous hope swelled in Alexis's chest and helped clear her muddled mind. She had to find a way to subdue Scott and his goon. She had to save both her and Tague.

"Keep going, Melinda."

Yes, she had to keep going. If Tague regained consciousness they might have a chance. A small chance against a madman and a giant. But she was clutching for any straw of hope now.

Scott would never get custody of Tommy after this. She would. She'd see the boy she loved so much grow up. And she'd tell Tague that she loved him. He'd been right all along. Scott would have never given up until she was dead. He had too much riding on her not being able to prove she didn't kill Lena.

Only she couldn't die. Not now.

"I've forgotten my lines," she said, stalling for time. "If I can have a glass of water, I might be able to remember them."

"Get her some water, Bronco. My wife is auditioning for the role of her life. She has to show me the fear. Lots of fear. Show me what you look like when you know you're going to die."

Bronco got off the sofa and went for the glass of water.

One of Tague's eyes slit open. He moved his hand slowly, sliding it into his pocket.

She sipped the water and then went back to the lines.

"'Please go away. Just turn and leave before you do something you'll regret. Let me live. Please, let me live.'"

"You're losing the emotion again, Melinda. Too much thinking. Not enough feeling."

Tague was slowly gaining consciousness. She saw it in his eyes and in the steadier movement in his body. Slight movements so that Bronco and Scott didn't pick up on them from their seats angled toward her and away from him.

"'Have you never loved a woman? If you have, how can you do this to me?'"

"Is that the best you can do, Melinda? Get my bat, Bronco. Ineptness deserves punishment." He grabbed Melinda's arm and slung her to the floor.

Tague jumped to his feet, his movements so jerky Alexis thought he might fall. That's when she glimpsed the pistol tucked in the palm of his hand.

She saw the bat coming at her from high above her head. It was in Bronco's hand.

She cringed as the bat swung and the gun went off.

Bronco crumbled and fell to the floor.

Scott grabbed the bloody bat and came at her. Fury burned in his eyes. The gun fired again. This time she crumbled to the floor with Scott.

A second later she was wrapped in Tague's safe, strong arms.

"I love you, Alexis. I love you so much. I don't ever want to let you go."

"I love you, too. When I thought you might be dead…"

He silenced her with a kiss. "I couldn't die and leave you to that perverted bastard."

Pain still wracked her body as she turned first to Bronco and then to Scott. "Are you sure they're dead? I don't want one of those horror story endings where they spring back to life."

"They both took a bullet to the front of the brain. They're dead. But eventually one of us has to let go and call 911."

"Just promise me that this movie has a happy ending," Alexis said. "That means you have to love Tommy, too. Are you ready to be a father?"

"I am, but not in Hollywood. How do you feel about Texas and being a rancher's wife?"

"As long as the rancher is you. Now are you ready for my good news?"

"That we're alive?"

"That Scott had filed for a divorce months ago. It became final yesterday."

"In that case, my forever is going to start right now."

And this time when his lips touched hers, the promise of a lifetime of love was in his kiss. She'd finally found the place where she belonged.

It was in Tague's arms.

Epilogue

Two months later

Carolina stepped out of the bright sunshine and through the shadowed doorway of the small chapel where she and Hugh had gotten married so many years ago. Birds had been singing in the trees that day just as they were now.

The sun had struck the stained glass windows at an angle that had made the exquisite paintings of the life of Christ come alive. The windows were the biggest change that had been made to the chapel since Hugh's great-grandfather had built it for his own wedding. The chapel, like the ranch, represented continuity and family and love.

Hopefully there would soon be another wedding in the chapel—but only if charges of murder were dropped against Alexis. She hadn't killed Lena Fox. She couldn't have. The only crime she was guilty of was loving Tommy. The Los Angeles police would have to see that.

So far, they hadn't. And they hadn't taken Alexis's word for the fact that Scott had admitted the crime. His fame had turned his death into a Hollywood circus and people were clamoring for Alexis to shoulder some of the blame.

If Hugh were here, he'd know what to say to ease the trepidation that had all of the Lamberts living in dread. But he wasn't here and he'd never be here again.

Carolina's thoughts went back to the horrible, rainy night when the small plane he'd been in had crashed in a West Texas thunderstorm. When she'd gotten the news that he was dead, she'd wanted to die, too. She'd wanted it so badly, she'd prayed for it. Thankfully, God didn't answer all prayers with a yes.

Though the pain of losing him was still almost unbearable at times, she was thankful for every day she had with her wonderful family.

Damien, Durk and Tague. All three of her sons were so very different, and yet they all had inherited Hugh's love for the land and his abiding faith in his fellow man. They, like her memories, were the part of Hugh that made every day a blessing.

Damien and Tague had both put their lives on the line for the women they loved. Hugh would have cautioned them about the risks they were taking, but he'd have been so very proud of them. And he'd have loved Emma, Alexis, precious Belle and adorable, precocious Tommy as she did.

If the murder charges against Alexis were dropped, Tommy would stay in the family. Lena's written wishes would be honored. As official stepmother, Alexis would be granted full legal guardianship.

And Carolina had to admit, she was glad the depraved Scott Jeffery Hayden was not Tommy's biological father. Though from what she knew of Lena Fox, it amazed her that she'd had the courage to go behind his back and purchase sperm while hiding the doctor's report from him that declared he was sterile.

But no matter whom his biological father had been, Tommy would be cherished and loved by all the Lamberts, especially by Alexis, always his mother in her heart.

Belle's mother was dead, as well, and her father's identity was still unknown. It would break all their hearts when the time came for them to give her up. For now, all they could do was shower her with love and treasure every moment they had with her. Emma and Damien were such loving parents.

Now if only Durk could find the woman he was meant to love for the rest of his life.

Carolina stepped back into the glaring sunlight and then took the short walk to the family cemetery where she'd laid Hugh to rest. She'd never looked into the casket, couldn't bear to see the mangled remains of her handsome, marvelous Hugh after the plane crash.

She knew he'd gone to meet his maker, yet she still took comfort from the grave site. She pulled the flower from her hair as she approached. Then she knelt and placed the white blossom on the grave.

"You'd be so proud of your sons, Hugh. And you'd love Emma and Alexis and delight in Belle and Tommy. I love you, Hugh. And I miss you very much."

Tears moistened her eyes as she stood and looked back at the chapel. If there was a wedding between Tague and Alexis, it would hopefully be a small family affair in the chapel.

But if she had her way, the wedding reception would be the grandest event the little community of Oak Grove or possibly even Dallas had ever seen.

The Lamberts needed a celebration of love.

TOMMY SQUEALED IN glee as Tague gave him a gentle push in the old tire swing his father had hung for him and his brothers when Tague was no bigger than Tommy. He didn't remember the event, but he'd heard about it—many times.

Damien had wanted a fancy swing set with a fort like his friends had. Their father had said no way. So he'd hung the tire and helped them build a tree-house fort. That, along with the rope for swinging into the swimming hole, had kept all three of them occupied for years. His dad had been a smart man.

Not that Tague wasn't likely to buy Tommy a swing set any day now. Times had changed. But…

"One day we'll build a fort together, Tommy. And go fishing and swimming and climb trees and play catch and…"

"My, don't you sound all fatherly today," Alexis interrupted, as she walked up to join them.

"The idea of fatherhood is growing on me."

She sat down cross-legged in a patch of clover. "But you definitely had reservations about marriage and fatherhood when we met."

"Sometimes a guy doesn't know what he wants until he finds it."

Tague slowed the swing and Tommy jumped off to go chasing after a butterfly. Tague went over and sat in the grass next to Alexis. She laid a hand on his thigh and he marveled at how her touch could still set him on fire.

But his love for her went so much deeper than the physical attraction. It was difficult to believe she could have endured all she'd been through and not have lost her zest for life or her capacity to love.

"I had a call from Detective Hampton just before I joined you and Tommy."

"Good news, I hope."

"Lena's death has officially been ruled a murder."

Apprehension settled like acid in his stomach. "Surely you're not suspected of killing her?"

"No. The evidence against Scott is solid enough that her murder has been attributed to him. I'm officially cleared of all charges."

He put an arm around her shoulder. "That's terrific news."

"It is, but it's difficult to believe that a man who had the world at his feet couldn't be happy with that. He had to keep pushing for more. To be considered a genius. To have a perfect son."

"And then he couldn't love that perfect son once he found out he wasn't Tommy's biological father," Tague said.

"And he felt compelled to kill the woman he'd chosen for the perfect mother as payback for tricking him into believing that Tommy was his son."

"And so that he could marry you," Tague reminded her.

"I was so caught up in my devotion and concern for Tommy that I fell into Scott's trap. It's a miracle that either Tommy or I escaped the madness. We wouldn't have had it not been for you, Tague."

"I only helped in the end, Alexis. You took Tommy and went on the run. You did what you had to do to keep him safe."

"But what makes a man who has everything keep pushing and pushing until he goes mad?"

"No one can answer that question, but in Scott's case

I'm sure his childhood, drugs and his hunger for power played into it."

"I guess I just have to accept that there are people like Scott Jeffery Hayden in the world. But the real marvel is that there are men like you in the world, too, Tague."

"I'm just a cowboy who happens to be crazy in love with you and can't wait to take you for my wife."

"And I love you more than I ever thought I could love anyone. So let's not wait any longer, Tague."

He pulled her into his arms and kissed her. The thrill went clear down to his toes. "Today works for me. I have a justice of the peace on speed dial."

"Liar. But I want a wedding in the family chapel like all the Lambert brides before me. I want it all, Tague. You, life on the ranch, the big, boisterous family."

"You're sure?"

"I've never been more certain of anything in my life." She jumped up, took his hand and tugged him to his feet. "C'mon, cowboy, let's go tell your mom that she's about to get a new grandson."

"Yee-haw," Tommy called from the top of a rock he'd just climbed.

Tague couldn't have said it better himself.

* * * * *

REQUEST YOUR FREE BOOKS!
2 FREE NOVELS PLUS 2 FREE GIFTS!

Harlequin®

INTRIGUE®

BREATHTAKING ROMANTIC SUSPENSE

Werewolf and elite U.S. Navy SEAL, Matt Parker, must set aside his prejudices and partner with beautiful Fae Sienna McClare to find a magic orb that threatens to expose the secret nature of his entire team.

Harlequin® Nocturne presents the debut of beloved author Bonnie Vanak's new miniseries, PHOENIX FORCE.

Enjoy a sneak preview of THE COVERT WOLF, available August 2012 from Harlequin® Nocturne.

Sienna McClare was Fae, accustomed to open air and fields. Not this boxy subway car.

As the oily smell of fear clogged her nostrils, she inhaled deeply, tried thinking of tall pines waving in the wind, the chatter of birds and a deer cropping grass. A wolf watching a deer, waiting. Prey. Images of fangs flashing, tearing, wet sounds...

No!

She fought the panic freezing her blood. And was gradually able to push the fear down into a dark spot deep inside her. The stench of Draicon werewolf clung to her like cheap perfume.

Sienna hated glamouring herself as a Draicon werewolf, but it was necessary if she was going to find the Orb of Light. Someone had stolen the Orb from her colony, the Los Lobos Fae. A Draicon who'd previously been seen in the area was suspected. Sienna had eagerly seized the chance to help when asked because finding it meant she would no longer be an outcast. The Fae had cast her out when she turned twenty-one because she was the bastard child of a sweet-faced Fae and a Draicon killer. But if she found the Orb, Sienna could return to the only home she'd known. It also meant she could recover her lost memories.

Every time she tried searching for her past, she met with a closed door. Who was she? Which side ruled her?

Fae or Draicon?

Draicon, no way in hell.

Sensing someone staring, she glanced up, saw a man across the aisle. He was heavily muscled and radiated power and confidence. Yet he also had the face of a gentle warrior. Sienna's breath caught. She felt a stir of sexual chemistry.

He was as lonely and grief stricken as she was. Her heart twisted. Who had hurt this man? She wanted to go to him, comfort him and ease his sorrow. Sienna smiled.

An odd connection flared between them. Sienna locked her gaze to his, desperately needing someone who understood.

Then her nostrils flared as she caught his scent. Hatred boiled to the surface. Not a man. Draicon.

The enemy.

Find out what happens next in THE COVERT WOLF
by Bonnie Vanak.

Available August 2012 from Harlequin® Nocturne
wherever books are sold.